I AM THE ONE

BY DD ANDER

AUTHOR'S NOTE

WHAT YOU ARE ABOUT TO READ IS A WORK OF FICTION EXTRACTED FROM THE FERTILE IMAGINATION OF THE AUTHOR. NO PART OF THE CONTENTS RELATE TO ANY REAL PERSONS, LIVING OR DEAD.

WEBSITE: www.ddander.com

EMAIL: duaneanderson507@gmail.com

ISBN: 978-0-9953193-4-9

DEDICATION

TO THOSE WHO FIGHT PREJUDICE WHEREVER IT REARS ITS' UGLY HEAD.

The Free Dictionary defines it thus:

Prejudice: 1. (a) The act or state of holding unreasonable preconceived judgments or convictions; (b) An adverse judgment or opinion formed unfairly or without knowledge of the facts

2. Irrational suspicion or hatred of a particular social group, such as race or adherents of a religion

3. (a) Detriment or harm caused to a person, especially in a legal case; (b) Preclusionary effect, preventing further pursuit of one's interests

TABLE OF CONTENTS

1.

AND SO IT BEGAN

Aaron did what Aaron always did. He just got up and left. And that was the last they saw or heard from him. The divorce had hit him hard; harder than anyone knew. Either he got the hell out of here or that gun he had stored away so long ago would be put to good use! He chose to leave.

There were rumours of course; someone had seen him here or there; or he was in trouble with the law, or he had committed suicide, or the 101 other things that people conjure up.

Those closest to him knew he wouldn't just disappear. That was totally out of character. Besides, he would have let them know. Wouldn't he?

Time passed by, and soon, even those closest to him, started to believe that either he lay dead somewhere yet undiscovered, or he had indeed left the country. He had often talked of his disdain for our way of life, and he had spoken fondly of some of the countries he had visited on his self dubbed "Journey of Discovery." Then he left. Could he really have just walked away? Without a word to anyone?

So what did happen? And where was he now? Would he not have been in contact if he were able to? He had always stayed in touch regardless of where he ventured.

How well do we really know each other? Really? How well do we even know ourselves? Do you know what you are capable of? Do you?

Aaron had never been the type to worry about fitting in. He just did. Some found his attitude to be somewhat arrogant, but, if they knew him at all, they would realize that it was confidence. And that he had in abundance.

It served him well. In all areas. In business, and definitely in his personal life! He had given up long ago trying to figure out what criteria women used in evaluating a man. All he knew for sure was that whatever it is he had, it worked. He wasn't about to spend a lot of time "getting ready" or standing in front of a mirror. A shower, a quick shave, a little dab of a good aftershave, a good deodorant, and clean clothes. Thank you very much!

He had little respect for those guys who spent as much time as a woman getting ready to go out.

Aaron's look, if that's what it was called, was casual. A sports jacket, blue jeans and a high quality shirt served him well. He had always worked out, and it showed. The only thing he knew for sure was that women liked confident men, and they were in short supply. And if you liked him, fine. If you didn't, well, that was fine too!

The divorce hit him harder than he had expected even though he wanted it as much as she did. But, all the crap that went with it! The accusations! My God! He had decided long ago to just shut his mouth. It wouldn't really matter anyway. People had already made up their minds, and anything he might say would just add fuel to the fire. To put it politely: some get the gold mine and some get the shaft! That's just the way it is!

He had never been one to keep up with the Jones, but in this area, and in the circle they travelled in, it was simple. More is better! After all, we work hard and we deserve everything that we get.

Ominous words indeed! Greed and need often become confused, and he had to admit, he had mixed them up on more than one occasion himself.

But still he had grown weary of the hypocrisy of so many of those around him, including himself. So perfect they were, heads bowed, eyes closed (depending on who was watching, of course). But, touch their pocketbook and a whole other persona would introduce itself unless there was a plaque attached to their names, or a dinner held in their honour. Give with your palm facing downward. Give with no expectation of return. Great words but seldom applied (unless it qualifies for a tax write off, of course). Woe to those who are "different" or down on their luck! Good luck with that! "Go to work" or "They're just lazy." Or "It's their own fault." He especially loved this one: "If I give my money away today, I might not have enough to live on 20 years down the road."

He had struggled these past years, mostly with himself. "Who am I? What do I stand for, if anything? Am I just kidding myself?"

And for good measure, or perhaps to add a little incentive to a decision already made, a friend of his was essentially led to slaughter by some upstanding citizens trying to protect their own asses from being exposed for the hypocrites they were. Better to shoot the messenger. And that's exactly what they did!

So Aaron made a decision. He didn't talk to anyone about it. That's not actually true. He and God had a little chat; pretty one sided as he recalled. What he didn't know at the time was that God decided to tag along!

And that's the way it went. He wasn't lonely. Alone, granted. But lonely? No.

But Aaron did it the typical Aaron way. He bought a map of Central/South America; he pinned it to the wall, grabbed a set of darts and proceeded to make his decision. He had 5 darts in total, and which ever country 2 or more darts landed on that's where his journey would begin. Simple as that!

And Mexico it was! So the die was cast and Cancun became home for a while. What a time he had! He wandered the streets at will, and he befriended the locals, and they him. At least most of them. But, there were others. They watched and they waited, and when the gringo left the pub that night alone, it was time. They beat him and dragged his limp body under the pier and left him for dead. Had it not been for a couple of kids searching for seashells the next morning, and then telling their parents, Aaron's journey may well have ended there. Three days later, he was released from the hospital, badly beaten but still alive. They had taken what money he had on him, but fortunately, he had left his gear at the hostel.

He did not share this with those back home. But he kept in touch, despite the rumours, mostly by email and blogs. He could not let them hear his voice for all would be revealed. So, he licked his wounds. He decided, then and there that this would never happen again, or, if it did, he would be ready!

This was not a violent man but he had become an angry man. This past year or so had not treated him well. Now this . . .

2.

THE CAMP

He knew the path he was about to take would take him into a world unlike anything he had ever known. He knew he was in a bad space. But he did it anyway. He had heard about a "training camp" through the local grapevine. No one would ever take advantage of him again if he had his way! It's amazing what a few dollars in the improper hands can accomplish. They picked him up, hood on head, and whisked him into a world where up was down and right was wrong.

He had taken some precautions. He had let his family know that he was on a voyage at sea and wouldn't be able to contact them for a few weeks. Don't worry, it's safe! That should take care of that. They would never know. And they didn't. It reminded him of another time, long, long ago when he had jumped on that bird and it had delivered him to the east coast. The seas had always attracted him and now he was going. And he did. He nearly died. How these people could do this job voluntarily, putting their very lives at risk on a daily basis was beyond him. Yet, here he was. Now, we're not trying to compare the two, but sliding down the deck of a stern troller and knowing that if the next wave doesn't catch soon, that burial at sea would be the reality. The wave caught . . . and by sheer determination, he was accepted into the fraternity. But danger was the constant password and it would rear its' ugly head on many occasions. A giant of a whale sealed the deal for our intrepid traveller, for visions of Moby Dick came alive in the flesh and he determined that if he got out of this alive, his seafaring career would be no more. They did survive, all but one, on this voyage, but when the gang plank hit the shore, he was gone!

Now he found himself at a camp in the remote jungles of Mexico. He had left a letter with a friend in Cancun that was to be sent to his family two months hence if he didn't return. He prayed that that letter would never be sent . . . It wasn't.

This is not what he had expected. Not at all! "I've changed my mind. Would you mind taking me back to my hotel, please?" As if that was going to happen! He realized right then and there that he may never see his family again. He'd better suck it up and fast. And he did.

At first it was difficult. Beyond difficult! He'd gotten in his fair share of scraps in his younger days, but nothing like this. In the days and weeks to follow, he would be beaten time and again. Over and over! With each beating he grew a little angrier, and he became a whole lot smarter.

Another day. Another beating being laid on him, and then it all changed. He still didn't know what the hell happened, but suddenly he was on top, and if they hadn't pulled him off, he would have killed that son of a bitch! That would be the last beating anyone at that camp would even come close to laying on him!

When he retired that night, he was surprised at how calm he was. When he emerged the next morning, and made his way to the mess hall, a path cleared before him. He had clearly won their respect. He was one of them now. They rejoiced and he cried inside.

There would be more beatings. By him. On them. He became feared. This passive gringo had changed, maybe even snapped. He talked little, but spoke volumes with his fists. Over the following weeks he mastered the art of the knife. And woe to those who put a gun in his hands. He may have come here to learn how to defend himself, but he would walk out of here a warrior.

There are many of these camps hidden in the jungles of Central and South America, and they have but one purpose. Train and recruit them to your causes. There is no shortage of damaged, would be warriors anxious to believe in anything, to be part of something, part of a family. Then there was Aaron. There were any number of takers for his services but he was determined to walk out of there as his own man. And he did. But he was warned. "Draw attention to us and we will find you and we will kill you. We will find your family and kill them too. Make no mistake about that!"

That should have been that! But, it wasn't. Marcos had recruiters in this camp as well as many other camps. When he heard about the gringo, he knew he had to have him. "This could be the piece of the puzzle I'm missing. Let him leave but follow him. I don't care where he goes. Just stay with him. He will be mine!"

Marcos had long awaited this day. One more piece of the puzzle had come home to roost. He could barely contain himself. A Canadian! Perfect! They may have driven him out of Panama years ago, but he had planned his return these past twenty plus years, and he was nearly ready to execute his plan. An American he would have settled for, but, a Canadian! There is a God! He would take him under his wing and school him. But first, let's get him to Panama!

To think that Aaron had come here voluntarily! He thought he was street smart. Man, he was nothing but a baby in this world! But, finally, he was out of there. And he knew he could handle whatever came his way.

Had he only known!

In most ways, he was the same friendly, compassionate character he had always been, but now there was an edge to this man, barely discernible, but there nonetheless. Woe to those who dared cross him. Get close but not to close if you were smart. Some did. Some didn't. And some became too close.

3.

MARIA

Her name was Maria. She was intelligent, she had personality plus and she was a beauty in her own right. She wanted to be with him. And he wanted to be with her. They danced the nights away, and they made plans. This gringo could and would fit in. Except he didn't.

When he had first seen her, she had literally taken his breath away. And that was strange for him. He was not the type to "stare" but everything from her flowing black hair to her olive complexion to those beautiful pouting lips drew him in as if a magnet. Her tiny waist only emphasized her ample breasts that much more. The white v neck blouse to the large belt to the flowing skirt, painted a moving picture of this elegant creature. She moved about as if slow dancing, and Aaron knew that she had indeed cast a spell over him.

There was nothing pretentious about Maria. She knew who she was and she dressed like she felt. That unnerved some and certainly caused a few stares but it didn't bother her one bit. That was their problem, not hers!

She was beautiful, no doubt, but it was her absolute joy of life that seduced Aaron. And he could not escape its grip. Nor did he try.

He had seen her at the bistro a few times, and it was obvious why the patrons returned time and again. She was intoxicating in every way. She served them all as if they were the most important person in the room. And her smile! He returned time and again just to watch her. But she was watching as well. There was something about this gringo. He wasn't like the others who treated her like she was for sale.

It finally happened. Outside the bistro. They literally bumped into each other at the market, and neither was about to let this pass. And they didn't. Soon they were enjoying more than coffee together. The two became as one, and they began to plan their future together. This had happened so quickly, yet it felt good, really good. She promised herself that she would tell him of her past; she didn't think he would care. He had to know that in her earlier years she had been part of a gang. At first it was cool, but as she had matured, she knew she had to get out, and follow her own dreams. Leaving the gang had never been allowed, but she had stood up to them, and they had made an exception. They let her go. But that did not sit well with the gang.

She knew she would always need to be wary. Now that she was involved with this gringo, she knew he must be told. If he loved her as he said he did, then they would get past this. So she told him. And that was that. Except it wasn't.

They came late one night when he was gone, and, when they left . . . This gringo would become well known in the days to come. Three Mexicans would not go home to their families again. And the community cheered. This gringo would not be forgotten. Yet, when the police came, they knew him not.

Then he moved on. Well, somebody moved on. He knew he couldn't go home and he didn't.

His very soul hung in the balance. And that's what they counted on.

Playa del Carmen welcomed him but he couldn't stay. Cozumel tried mightily to seduce him, and it did for a time. The diving was great; the parties endless; the acceptance complete. But, as he looked around, he saw himself replicated, and he could not stay. One of him was more than enough. So he left. Again. Try as he might, sleep was not his friend. Maria came to him in the night and comforted him as best she could. He cried out to her and he cried out to God, but comfort came not.

4.

A MARKED MAN

He had caught their interest in the camp. He wasn't one of them. Yet he was there. He was good. Very good. Possessed even. And angry at the world. Perfect.

Though he had went to the camp to better protect himself in the future, this decision would begin to define this man. If this man believed in anything, it would be severely tested in the days to come.

So he was shadowed from the moment he left the camp and they would begin to shape this man. He wouldn't know, but they would. So they watched and they waited. They knew he had been beaten severely in the weeks preceding his stay in the camp. They knew now what they had to do. When he took up with Maria, her fate was sealed. And his would be too. Three Mexicans had been well paid for their "work." He had done as they predicted and now he was theirs. Unknown to him.

They would let him travel as he would. They would set up scenarios as required. But he had to remain unaware of their presence. He mixed well with gringos and locals alike. People liked this guy and they wanted to keep it this way. Now he was in Cozumel. They needed him to move on.

They would wait a little longer. If he didn't move on soon, they would have to "arrange" something. But he did move on. Their intelligence had been right. Belize would soon be his home.

Ultimately he would make his way to Panama. Then they could execute their plan. But he needed to be tested a few more times. That, they could arrange.

Sleep had finally found its' way to this man. So, at long last he rested and the nightmares spared him, at least for a time. He found that strange. He had crossed a line, not once, but three times, and it bothered him not. He wondered if he could ever go home again. Had he forfeited his soul?

But something was wrong. He felt like he was being watched. He would find himself glancing about or turning quickly to look behind him. Yet there was never anyone there. As much as he would try to shrug it off, he knew something was amiss.

5.

ANGELINA

He loved Belize , especially Caye Caulker. And he began to relax. He caught himself laughing, my God, laughing! When had he last laughed? But it would not last. He knew it. When Angelina came into his life, he was afraid. Afraid for her. He could not bear to lose her as he had Maria.

Stop it! That was Mexico! Maria had made some bad choices earlier. Once you're in, you're in.

She was in. Now she was out. Now three of them were out as well. And he had left. They could have been good together, these two. He had mourned, for a time, and then he had moved on.

Quickly. Too quickly, even for him, and he was confused.

Angelina was special. If there was ever to be an ambassador for her country, it should have been her. This is a poor country and the orphanage system is abominable. She is determined to set it right. If sacrifice is required, so be it. When Aaron first met her, he thought little of it. She managed the place he was staying at; she was super efficient, and all business. He gave it little thought, if at all. Maria's tragic death had thrown him into despair and he cared little about anything. He needed rest and this quiet little retreat would serve him well.

But then he started to really notice her. After work she let her hair down and relaxed a little. As they began to engage in conversation more and more, Aaron began to pay more attention to her. Her passion for life could not be contained, and soon he became excited about their nightly chats. And as much as he didn't want to, he began to really look at her. And he liked what he saw. Those eyes! Beautiful! She was several years younger than him, but that didn't bother her in the slightest. And when she suggested they spend some time together on her day off, he could find no reason not to. And that was that.

She may have been five feet tall, all one hundred and ten pounds of her. Again, as with Maria, her hair fell to her shoulders, and the tank top and shorts on this day accented her curvaceous body. Funny, he hadn't really noticed that before, but then, he hadn't really looked! But now, despite feeling guilty that he was even looking so soon after Maria, he began noticing a lot.

She liked being with him. And she told him so. She knew he had had a recent tragedy in his life so she didn't push too hard. At least at first. But, they were so good together and she began to think about their life together. It didn't take long for him to get on board . . . but . . . these ominous feelings were overwhelming, and he knew this would not end well.

They would talk for hours on end. She would share her dreams, and she would come alive! It was contagious to all those around her. "Join me" she would plead. Let's do this together! For a time, he believed it was possible. They had such fun together. They frolicked as if they were children. They dove with the sting rays and they searched the mangroves for the elusive manatees. It was good. He began to imagine their life together. Such a beautiful place and such a beautiful woman. My God. Who wouldn't want this? And he did. But, it was good with Maria as well, wasn't it?

He grew uneasy. Something was wrong. He knew it. Call it a "gut" feeling or sixth sense or whatever, but if he was indeed being watched, then so was she. He would not have her end up as Maria.

So he began to withdraw from this woman. And she became angry. "I thought you were different. I thought you loved me!"

He did love this woman. But he was scared for her. Paranoid? Perhaps. But he could not bear to lose her. But lose her he would, but at least she would be alive.

So he moved on once again. But this time he would be the observer. He knew not who to observe but he knew he was right. And they knew that he was on to them. They retreated into the shadows and they knew their job had become much harder.

Still he sent emails and blogs to his loved ones. And assured them that all was well. They believed him. Yet, there were questions, and those that knew him well knew that there was much contained between the lines. And stay between the lines they would if he had his way.

They wanted him to come home for a while but he could not. He knew not why but he was compelled to continue this journey. And that is what he would do. He missed Angelina dearly but he dared not get in touch. Perhaps he was wrong, and if so, it would be a regret he would take to his grave. But something was terribly wrong; and that, he knew for sure!

So Barton's Cave became his destination. Now, this should have been simple enough, but, in his world, nothing was simple anymore. He had heard about these caves and now he could finally go exploring. It was as they had said. Once again he had to go outside his comfort zone to take this trip. He was alone with the guide and they were heading deep into the jungle . OK. But then he stopped and picked up another local. Two of them; and him. Here we go again. But this time he was ready. They were great guys and he began to relax. Until he met Nick.

6.

INDIANA JONES GONE WRONG

What a piece of work! Indiana Jones gone wrong! Big, hairy and sweaty and carrying an AK 47. Crap! And a mouth to match. And he was mad. "What the hell do you think you're doing? Why are you here? I've shot people for less! Talk! Now!"

Our man had nothing to say. A gun pointed in his face by some flipping lunatic. A guide cowering on the ground. And him. He could feel himself tense up, and he knew this would not end well for one of them.

He didn't shut up! He bragged about how many people he had killed. No one would ever take advantage of him again! "So, what to you have to say for yourself, asshole?"

And then it was too late. Perhaps he had trained for only a few weeks but he had been trained well. "Indiana Jones" would rule no more. The police were called, and once again, no one saw or heard anything. And "Nick" didn't have a clue what happened, only that it wasn't these guys. They had found him lying unconscious and aided him as best they could. They called the police. If not for them . . .

This would not be the last time this would happen to this man. So, a simple pleasure trip turned into a nightmare once again. What the hell happened back there? Well, it turned out that something had indeed happened. About two years ago, according to the guide, "Nick" had staked out this area and denied access to the caves. This pissed off the locals and the war was on. And indeed, Nick had shot several men. Accused them of trying to steal what was his. Steer a few bucks into the proper hands and he had no worries. Down here, happens all the time. Well, not this time. He had met his match on another occasion as well. About a year ago. Except this time one of the locals took a machete to him. He nearly died, but he didn't. If he was paranoid before, well, now he was impossible. But, one day he would meet someone who wouldn't take his crap, and today just happened to be that day.

But still, hero or zero, Aaron knew he had better get out of the country. Now! So he was on the move again! Guatemala welcomed him and Florence became his home for a time. Looks great. Picturesque for sure. But, as he was finding on this "journey of discovery" everything was not as it appeared. Or was it just him?

Marcos' men hadn't forgot about him. In fact, they knew what he had "done" to Nick. And they knew he was on the move again. He was proving to be even more than they had hoped for. It appeared "scenarios" weren't going to be needed all that often as he was doing a fine job all by himself. Though he would never know it, his decision to leave Caye Caulker had probably saved a young lady's life. Their job was made easy by this Canuck gone wild. But, if and when they had to step in, rest assured, they were more than up to the task. So they stayed close, always just out of the periphery of this man.

Sleep became hit and miss once again. Visions of Maria and her horrible death haunted him. And what of Angelina . . . would she have suffered the same fate? And why? Maybe he was just a coward. Commitment? Not his strongest suit! But still, he sensed that something was amiss. He knew not what it was, but it hung in the air and threatened to suffocate him.

7.

GUATEMALA BECKONS

Tikal had always spoken to him and now he would engage this place of mystery in person. Tikal made Chichen Iza feel like a walk in the park. Dark, foreboding, and dangerous, the jungles of Guatemala threatened to devour them. Without question, its inhabitants would if they were foolish enough to stray from its' paths. Those who had in the past had paid dearly for their transgressions. As he followed this group up into the jungles to catch the setting sun from the top of the pyramid, he could not help but notice that once again, guns and guards were ever present. Gun of choice: sawed off shotgun. Now, were they there to guard these would be adventurers or were they there to ensure these adventurers didn't get out of hand? Perhaps to guard us again the denizens of the jungle? If you thought that, you'd be wrong. Interestingly enough, once the graft had passed their hands, they became conspicuous by their absence. Jaguars prowled within feet of their path and howler monkeys screamed out at them. Chills ran down their spines. Stuck in the jungle late at night with a headlamp for a companion, and a bunch of tourists, certainly did not inspire confidence. They rose at 4 a.m. to once again tackle the pyramids and catch the jungle coming alive as the sunrise burst over the horizon. Of course, the money changers greeted them that morning, collected their bounty and disappeared once again. Big surprise! At least these enemies he could see and he was comforted by that thought. But still he was uneasy. Paranoid or not, something was not right.

He had planned on catching the bus out of Florence later that night. He figured he might as well do an overnighter to Guatemala City. Might as well save the cost of a room, and besides, when he got to the city, he would just catch a shuttle to Antigua. Or so he thought. Turned out his plan wasn't so good. At least, according to the locals. Apparently that highway crossing the country attracted a lot of attention. From thieves, and if you were a foreigner, a possible kidnapping. Especially at night. Cancel that plan! So instead he caught a flight. The bus would have been a 12 hour plus trip across a foreboding landscape but he was prepared to suck it up. But, add "possible kidnapping" and it was a no brainer.

Guatemala City. Surreal. Drive through those streets and you will have tales to tell, provided you live. He had picked a particularly bad time to arrive in the city. Of course, he didn't know that, but the "mafia" had a few points to make. The best way to do that is to panic the public. Most of the working class relies on the bus system. On a normal working day, one bus driver is murdered daily, usually over drugs, but he had won the lottery. Four or five bus drivers each day were being murdered. Why? To paralyze the city. To create chaos. In a city of 3 million people, and the system grinding to a halt, the government would be driven to their knees, again, and they would control the city. Happens all the time. 100 murders plus weekly in this country! Welcome!

So, fortunate he was, as a shuttle full of other tourist types picked him up, and the driver displayed his NASCAR skills and worked his magic. Oblivious they were to the chaos and broken bodies only one block away.

But they were headed to Fantasyland . . . sorry, Antigua. Purported to be a "crown jewel" in this land gone wrong. Indeed, at first glance, it is all that. Surrounded by mountains, Spanish architecture, cobblestone streets, it is easy to forget that this is also a violent place. But most have brought along their ivory coloured glasses and Fantasyland welcomes them!

To reiterate: over 6000 murders per year; put another way, app. 43 for every 100,000 residents. (Canada, by comparison, has 1.6 for every 100,000 residents); 97% not even investigated; considered one of the best places in the world to murder someone and not get caught. Perhaps it was time to set our "friend" up for some action.

He was there! So were they! And it was time to up the ante!

He had been told about the People's Hostel, and as it turned out, they had a private room available. So once again, home sweet home! Time to make a few calls home to let them all know what a great time he was having. Email a few cool photos, write an upbeat blog and everyone would be happy. That's the way he wanted it. And that's the way it was. At least for now. The cobblestone streets, the pastel coloured buildings, wrought iron fences and gates everywhere invited everyone in. The central park was always alive with performers and the colourful clothing of the indigenous a sight to behold. Language students and their teachers were everywhere. Not a care in the world for these fine folk. Really?

And there was Volcan Pacaya. Last eruption, 2010, but dangerous still today. A view from the summit was breathtaking, and as long as you kept moving, your shoes wouldn't melt. And tough to climb. So much volcanic shale . . . two steps forward, one step back, but worth the toil. But there was another element at work here; thieves actively worked these areas and most tours arranged to have guards along. Tourists were often targeted; if they dared stray they were fodder for the roaming gangs and some of these were incredibly violent. The operator on this particular tour was extremely well paid to alter his tour just a little (and it wasn't by the tourists).. So when this group took a wrong turn partway down the mountain, no one thought it peculiar. After all, their guide knew the mountain. He knew what he was doing. Nothing to worry about.

8.

SETUP

Then it happened. There were three of them. Masked and armed heavily and waiting for them. Crap! For a bunch of tourists? What the hell! This didn't make any sense! They were on the mountain; all their belongings were in the van down below. And they weren't going there. So all they got were nickels and dimes, big deal! Then they started releasing their hostages: that couple there, an obvious college group, a couple of older guys, and the guide. And him? No way! No way was this a robbery and over the next couple of hours he would be beaten again and again. Visions of yesterday swept over him. He knew he had been right all along. He was a target. Had been for a long time. And he got angry. That's what they were counting on. They had instructed the gang to beat this man, and then dump him close to his hotel. If they were right, he'd make it back to the hotel and they wouldn't.

A phone call tipped the police off and when they arrived they found a package waiting for them. Neatly wrapped but badly broken. And they had nothing to say. Three more gang members were in custody. As usual, no witnesses. Whoever had done this to these punks deserved a medal, but of course, that wasn't going to happen.

He'd lost it. Again. But now he was convinced that this attack, like the others, was calculated, and he was the mark. But why? He began to think back. Maria had been slaughtered . . . because of him? He had taken care of that "problem." He "knew" that Angelina was in danger . . . now he was sure of it ."Oh my God, if I had stayed, she'd probably be dead by now." A chill ran down his spine and he gasped for air less he suffocate. Why? It makes no sense! Then there was "Nick." They couldn't have arranged that, no way! And now, these punks! Actually, it made perfect sense, just not to him. But what they didn't know was that now he knew, and one day they would pay. Dearly!

He stayed on in Antigua for a few more days. Wary but indignant. And he watched. Everyone. If they were watching him, whoever the hell they were, he would be watching right back. If they revealed themselves, then, this would not end well . . . for them!

So he kept his routine simple and he sat where he could observe everyone. No one escaped his gaze. If they were here, he would ferret them out. Three more days would pass and he became frustrated. Maybe he was just being paranoid after all. No! No chance! He wasn't a spy, but he was sure he would spot something or someone acting suspicious. Nope.

Fine. He felt good enough to travel and he was determined to continue on this so called "journey to anywhere but here." The hell with them.

So he caught the shuttle to the City and boarded the bus: destination, San Jose, Costa Rica. El Salvador would have to wait. But, the way this journey had gone so far, who knows?

Wise words indeed. There would be stories. But, told to him, not about him. Pablo was a God send . He was finding the language difficult and then a tap on his shoulder. He immediately tensed and prepared himself. This might be them! But it wasn't. And it didn't take long to figure it out. Someone actually wanted to help him with no strings attached. Really? Really! They talked and they shared and Pablo told him his story. How his father had been murdered and dumped unceremoniously in the dump; he was just one of many who happened to be on the wrong side when "they" came. Or how his uncle pastored the largest congregation in the City, and how he stood tall among the chaos, a beacon of hope in these trying times. And how he and his family were forced to abandon their family business because they would not bend to the will of the drug lords who controlled 85% of all business done. They had their values, and although forced to abandon their dream, they chose life. But at least they could sleep at night with a clear conscience.

Now, he was with this gringo approaching San Salvador. They had become fast friends, and before he headed out to the work site, they shared a pizza from, of all places, Pizza Hut! As they walked along the street they were under constant guard until he was back at his hotel.

This is a land under constant attack, either from nature itself or almost continuous war. They say "death squads" still roam these areas. Pablo was not comfortable here, nor were most of the people he met in the following days. Except one. A Canadian photographer who either knew something no one else did, or was just plain nuts. And probably dead by now.

So he spent the next 10 hours at the hotel awaiting the next bus. He sat out on the balcony . . . his constant companion a guard with a sawed off shotgun. He moved, the guard moved.

It would take another 20 hours to reach San Jose. Constant stops by armed guards were their greeting party. When they crossed the border into Nicaragua, it became apparent that there would be no relief for some time to come. And there wasn't.

9.

EL SALVADOR, NICARAGUA, COSTA RICA

What a long, hard haul. And now another stop at the Nicaragua border. Hot, dirty, and smelly were these travellers but there would be no relief for many more hours. Even more border guards, and even more guns awaited. Suspicious of everyone, all the time. That can make for itchy fingers. And mayhem.

So they dug out their luggage again, and hauled it over to the long dusty table that seemed to be set up in such a fashion to cause maximum discomfort. As the sun beat down on them relentlessly, the guards shuffled and seemed eager to stir something up. With his luck recently, it would be him, no doubt. But, it wasn't. As they stood in line, he'd watched this old indigenous lady struggle with her oversized suitcase, and finally, he went over and took it from her and threw it up on the table. Two guards, watching this, came over to them, chatted among themselves for a moment, indicated to him that he was to grab his luggage, and they were both escorted across the border. "Go!" And he was gone.

An hour later, when the rest had been let through, a French Canadian couple came over to him. "Who are you? The same thing happened at the last stop. We all stand in line and they just let you through. He had to chuckle. It was true. Things happened like that all the time to him. But on this trip there was a lot of crap happening as well. And that was strange. Coincidence? He didn't believe in coincidence and he knew he wasn't being paranoid either.

Once again, this didn't go unnoticed. Once again this gringo had walked through security like they weren't even there. And that would definitely work to their advantage. They were there and he didn't know. Perfect.

Finally, after what seemed forever, San Jose presented itself. Thank God! Twenty hours from San Salvador. By bus! 8 hours by bus from Guatemala City to San Salvador. 28 hours seat time! Never again!

After checking in with their chief, the "followers" were relieved of their duties and a fresh set of eyes was assigned to this man. "Stay close to him until he gets into Panama. Find out his itinerary. It doesn't matter if it's a week or a month. Just stay with him and make sure he crosses the border. Then he's ours!"

Had he known what was in store for him, he would have got on a plane and headed to the other side of the world. But he didn't know. And he didn't go.

San Jose did nothing for him so he headed up into the cloud forests of Santa Elena and Monteverde. Another gruelling trip but definitely worth it. Rain galore. Why not just call this rain forests instead? Simple: rain forests get around 7 feet of rain each year; cloud forests only get about 3 feet! Funny! Like it made any difference how wet you got or not. Interestingly, the rain in this area blows sideways. Layout of the mountain passes or something like that. But, the zip lining was amazing, the rappelling spectacular, and hiking through the cloud forests unforgettable. He was actually enjoying himself. No worries. No stress. None. Was he finally free of this jinx or whatever it was that was following him around?

But all good things must end and soon he was on the move again. How about Montezuma? Kind of a hippie flavour to the place, they say. Laid back. Right on the Pacific side. You bet!

This would be interesting. As he headed towards the ferry that would deliver him to his destination, she joined him. "Pardon me. How about we hook up for a while? At least until we get there. Safety in numbers. "Why not? She had been a high powered executive in New York City, but one day she had had enough, and just walked away, and kept walking. And here she was, seven months later and still "finding herself." Sally and he hit it off instantly and shared many a meal together over the following days. They agreed that they really weren't backpackers but "flash packers." Backpackers with laptops, iPads , and other such gadgets that they couldn't live without. If and when they chose, they could stay in a fine hotel, or order up a gourmet meal. Such was their life. Rarely a tourist, always a traveler , but a budget that would allow for both. It was good. No further incidences. Maybe all the foolishness was over.

But it was time for him to go. She was not in danger, apparently. So go now before he became too attached to her, or she to him. All's well that ends well, and this had ended well indeed. So he caught a boat headed to Jaco where he would be unceremoniously dumped on the side of the road. Stranded again! Not the first time! He doubted it would be the last! And it wasn't!

Jaco it was. Not a place you want to be dumped in according to those in the know. But at least it was daylight, but daylight down south can disappear in a flash. Well, no use whining about it. Besides, there was no one to whine to!

10.

BILL AND SARAH

So he headed off down the street. Surely he wasn't the only one that had met his fate. And he was right. There they stood. Could have spotted them a mile off. Suitcases as big as they were. Obviously gringos. Much as he was sick of gringos, now was not the time to be picky. Safety in numbers!

They hit it off immediately. Bill and Barb had flown in for a wedding and, like him, had been dumped on the side of the road. They had been to the wedding and were now headed to Manuel Antonio, or so they thought. Turned out the driver didn't know that! In any case, there they were, and there he was. And he was headed pretty darn close to where they were going. So heads were put together, and with a little recruiting of the others gathered there, they were able to negotiate with a shuttle driver, and they were on their way. Turned out these two were Canucks, from Saskatchewan!

She read, and the men talked, and by the time this couple was dropped off, they had agreed to meet the next day. Barb wanted to get to the beach, get in a comfortable lawn chair, and read and relax. He wanted some adventure, and this guy he had just met seemed to fill the bill.

So they got her situated and off they went. The National Park is an absolute must, and remember, they were just tourists, doing touristy things. It was great. And it was fun. This guy was interesting, and alive, and that's exactly what he needed. But, he still glanced over his shoulder from time to time, and he found himself checking out others along the way. Just because nothing had happened in a while, didn't mean it wouldn't.

They frolicked as children, these grown men. Body surfing, you bet! Full bore! And beat up they were, these warriors! But there was no wave they wouldn't challenge, and,at least in their own minds, they were the great conquerors!

He began to talk of moving on. Panama was calling his name. And it was powerful. He had to go. Man, they would love to go to Panama, but they were leery. Everything they had heard . . . and that border crossing was supposed to be ugly, but the Panama Canal was so close, and Bocas del Toro; would love to check that out! This stranger they had just met was going anyway, and he was going alone, and he had invited them along. He was confident, cocky almost, but he had been down a lot of dangerous roads already, and if his stories could be believed, everything would fall into place. And they liked this guy! What the hell! We may not get this opportunity again! So they went for it! Now, he hadn't told them about the "other stuff" but that shouldn't really matter, should it?

So they made their way to the border. It was everything they had heard about. And worse. He had told them: be like sheep here, don't smile at, or try to engage the guards; absolutely no pictures. If you're right, and they're wrong about something, suck it up. Stay close and don't talk. Keep moving ahead. Don't look back. What the hell else? Over done a bit? Turned out, no! They were pulled aside, these three, and tossed into a room away from prying eyes. The interrogation began . . . and then it stopped, immediately. Someone had waved the guard over, and they conversed for a minute or so, and then they were told to pack their stuff and get the hell out of there. "What just happened?" "Bill, don't talk. Don't do anything.

Let's go. Remember what I said." And move they did. Until the next set of guards . . . check the passports again . . . move on . . . and again. Now . . . Breathe! "Why did they stop searching us? Why did they let us go?" It doesn't matter. Forget it. That's how it goes down here. At least this time!

So he was right all along. But still . . . And they would overnight in David. Little did he know how prominently David would figure in his life. Ultimately, it would become the pivot point of all that was to follow! And there was much more to follow!

The "followers" contacted their boss. They had to pull a few strings this time, but a few bucks goes a long way to making guards so much more agreeable. They had spent too much time and resources to get him to Panama to have it screw up now. And soon, the boss himself would take over, personally, and at long last the puzzle would be complete! As far as they were concerned.

So David would board and feed them this night, this trio of travellers. The best way to describe David: Hot! It may even be the hottest city in Latin America. It's a gateway city on the Pan American highway, in Chiriqui province, an agricultural hub, and only 45 minutes from the Costa Rican border. Why anyone would voluntarily live here, who knows! And yet, this would become his pivot point. This would be the place he would return to time and time again. This is the place he would attempt to build a life.

So they explored David and joined the crowds who gather day and night in Miguel de Cervantes Saavedra Park, definitely the gathering place in downtown David. He would grow fond of this place and it would begin to define him in so many ways.

11.

THE PUPPET MASTER

The next day they would board the Tica Bus bound for Panama City. On this bus, and on this day, his life would be forever changed. For on this bus he would meet the "puppet master" and he would enter a world that even he, with his vivid imagination, could not have envisioned.

Uneventful this trip began, and they edged ever closer to Panama City. His fellow travellers became worried. "We've heard so much about this place. Are you sure it's safe? We don't even have a place to stay. What if something happens? How do we know where to go? They could take us anywhere and we wouldn't know." Of course, they were right. That could happen. But, this trip was far from over yet, and if he was right, and so far, he had been, something would happen or someone would come along to help them out. Every time. So he didn't worry. He didn't have to; they were worried enough for all of them!

Then it happened! As always. The child sitting next to him was whisked away by his mother to be closer to her, and he was promptly joined by another passenger who had kindly given up his seat so mom and child could be together. And, he spoke english. Well. His friends looked over at him, shook their collective heads, and knew that this would all work out. If only they had his confidence!

He and Marcos exchanged pleasantries and then they began to talk. And talk! Soon these two were as old friends and the conversation flowed freely. Marcos told him about his life, and about his country, and about how he and his family had been forced to flee for their very lives. This was the time of Noriega, and Marcos was on the wrong side. He was an influential business man in his time, and he had spoken out. That was his down fall. He became a marked man, and that meant death, not just for him, but for his family as well. So they fled to the US and they forfeited everything. Everything they had worked so hard to achieve was gone! Everything! And he vowed that one day he would have his revenge . . . "Sorry, I'm talking too much. Tell me about you and your friends." So he did; short version, mind you, as Panama City had suddenly because visible to the naked eye. And his friends were getting anxious, again! "Marcos, I hate to impose, but we're really stuck. We don't have a clue where to begin or where to go, and as you can see, my friends are a little jumpy."

When they pulled into the terminal, they knew he would help them out. Thank God Marcos had happened along. And that those two had gotten along so famously! So he arranged a taxi for them, as well as a hotel for them to stay at, plus gave him all his numbers so that they could stay in contact. What a great guy! He had been right, as usual!

Marcos commanded attention. And he got it. Not large in structure: maybe 200 pounds, five foot nine inches or so, a pudgy, reddish complexion, but his presence cast a long shadow. He demanded respect. And he got it. One had the sense that this was not a person you dared cross. Aaron would soon find out that truer words were never spoken! Marcos was well spoken in both Spanish and English, and he could easily disarm those around him. It was not hard to see why he had been so prominent in his earlier years. Now he was back, and soon the world would know of this man. Just not now!

It was a great hotel. Hell, when they walked into the hotel, there was already a phone call waiting for him. "Just checking to make sure you arrived safely. Talk to you later!" Wow! You couldn't even make up this stuff! Right down town, walking distance to some great shops, and they felt good, and safe. When they discovered the pool on the roof top, well, it was good. Very good, and they relaxed. Tomorrow, they were headed for the Panama Canal!

They had rooms next to each other; they travelled together, yet apart. He respected their privacy, and they respected his. And that was a good thing. For who could have known that the room next to his would once again offer up a temptress. Not the room, of course, but it's' occupant. They met out on their respective balconies. She, a sea farer, a child of the universe. Ingrid was her name and she was passing through, bound for who knows where. And alone. They hit it off. Immediately. They would dine well that night. And share many a story. Perhaps they could hook up for a while. Perhaps. But in the wee hours of the morn, he boarded a bus, along with his friends, and headed to The Canal. When she knocked on his door that morning and there was no answer, she knew. And she moved on. Alone.

Marcos was mighty proud of himself. What a job he had done, thank you very much! And the "traveller" was his. If they had thought he was onto "them," well, put that to rest! Now he was in Panama! "My turf." and the "puppet master" laughed aloud. It had taken a couple of months of patience and some manipulation to get him here, but it had worked. What a stroke of luck! To find someone like him in a "training camp." What the hell was he thinking going to a place like that? When he first got the call, he couldn't believe it. A gringo, smart at that, and a very quick study, and apparently mad at the world, and no military connections to boot, was almost too much to ask for. Christmas came early, and if he worked this right, there would be a few people that definitely wouldn't see Christmas next year. Yes! It was good. Very good!

When Marcos and his cohorts escaped the clutches of Noriega so very long ago, they vowed that the fight was far from over. They would have their day in the sun. One day they would return. When Noriega fell, some of them made their way back to Panama. In the ensuing years they would begin to infiltrate the political parties of the day, and slowly but surely begin to exert their influence.

But it was not easy. The political spectrum of the day dismissed these so called patriots as yesterdays' men and they were relegated to the sidelines. They grew angrier and more determined than ever that one day they would be the rightful heirs. To hell with the lot of you! Patient they would be. In Panama that is a good quality. The people would eventually tire of all the political infighting. Each party and each politician trying to out do the other. Even more corrupt than that which went before them. That's the way it goes down there. And not just there. Promises would be made. Promises would be broken. Governments would change. As usual, the people would suffer. Not the top 10%, mind you! Just the rest.

Doors would be thrown wide open to the foreigners. Bring us your money. Grease our palms. And we will gladly sell our people down the drain! And come they did!

The indigenous would be the big losers. As usual. They would be pushed back further and further. Their lands would be plundered and raped under the watchful eye of their own powers that be. The millionaires club would become the billionaires club. Life was good. For the chosen few. And hell for the rest.

So Marcos and company would pursue their dreams. These powerful men, though snubbed by the politicians of the day, had very deep roots and had not lost sway among the older generation. The ones with money. Lots of it. The elitists. So they continued to raise funds and make plans for a New Panama. Their Panama. They would use the common man to make it a reality. Make them believe that this is for them. Pit the government of the day against the indigenous and the common man. Add in the foreign nationals. Stir them up. Then ride in on their great white horse to save the day. It would happen. And sooner than anyone expected if Marcos had his way!

12.

DOUBT NO MORE

All those doubts Aaron had earlier were starting to subside, and he was enjoying the companionship of these new friends. And he relaxed and put his fears aside. That Marcos. What a great guy! They would definitely be seeing more of each other in the future. Bet on it! Bet on it he should have, and he should have bet a lot! Guaranteed win, but the prize would not be to his liking.

So they headed to the Canal. After all, it's impossible to go to Panama and not do the Canal. They boarded what looked to be the oldest vessel there. But, as usual, there would be more to the story! It seemed a rather infamous character had owned this boat at one time. None other than, Al Capone! Yep! THAT Al Capone! The Canal was great, and he mingled with everyone, especially the ladies. He just couldn't seem to help himself! Bill would comment later "I felt like I was your wing man, but you definitely don't need one!" Interesting! The last thing he wanted was to get involved with another woman! Forget that! And he didn't. But he could have. He had taken down a few numbers and promised to keep in touch.

They explored the Canal, and they explored the "Old City" and the New, and they marvelled at its' architecture. But they knew it was a facade, for behind those walls, another world existed, and it would eat them up, dare they enter.

So they didn't. They played two days longer and then they departed. Bocas del Toro was speaking to them, and the thought of dipping their toes into the Caribbean would not be denied! So began another bus trip that would make them second guess their stay in Panama. And it would take place near Santiago.

He wasn't used to traveling with others. Now decisions would be shared and he would find himself acquiescing a lot more than he normally would have. But, that was ok for now. He had no intention of being a third wheel for long. Soon Santiago showed itself. Some lunch and off they went. Next stop, David. Except it wasn't. And once again the plot would thicken.

13.

UPRISING

They stood shoulder to shoulder, and behind them stood hundreds more, arms crossed and defiant. The Pan American highway would not grant passage this night. The indigenous of Panama would stand united against the foreign intruders who would rape and plunder their land. With the consent of their own government. They were becoming more organized and better funded, and much of the world was beginning to hear their voice. If they were to have their say, the time was now! Their bus would sit idle for many hours to come. Finally, in a last defiant act, a bonfire was set ablaze in the middle of the highway and the natives stepped aside to allow passage to the thousands of stranded motorists. Throughout Panama, in the days and months to come, their voice would become ever louder. Though he knew nothing of their plight, he would become a prominent figure in this struggle for the rights of these people.

14.

KARENA

So David it was once again. Another night in this town compliments of an uprising. Go figure! He was getting to know this town, particularly the town square known as Cervantes Park. He would visit this place many, many times in the months to come.

Finally, the bus was en route to Bocas, and the Caribbean was waiting! His friends were anxious. Again. Through the highlands they would go; beautiful rolling hills, waterfalls, and rivers greeting them at every turn.

Once again, a local came along side and helped these travellers find their way, until she arrived at her own destination. Now they were heading further and further into the jungle and soon they would have to navigate the waterways that would ultimately take them to their final destination. Again, as usual, someone would step forward and take them by the hand and lead them to the promised land.

What a job she did. From the bus to the taxi to the boats, to Bocas, and finally, another water taxi to Red Frog Beach. She had heard these travellers stressing out over where they were supposed to go once they reached Bocas, and phoned ahead to the resort where she worked. They had space available, and she had decided she might as well lead them all the way home. Thank God for Karena!

She had helped them get to Bocas, and now they were shopping for supplies,and she was ordering him about . . . do this, do that . . . and he told her so. "You are so flippin' bossy!" Bad move! He was just joking but he had forgotten to mention that little fact to her! That night, she would make him eat those words.

Feisty or what? She wouldn't take his crap and she was going to let him have it with both barrels.So they settled in, and later that evening they sat around the common area soaking it all in. When Karena's shift ended, she came over to chat with her new friends. Well, two of them were friends. Him, not so sure. She lit into him. "How dare you talk to me like that! I was helping you and you called me bossy! And you completely ignored me!" She was peeved and he was going to know it! He laughed at her. Wrong thing to do! She got even more upset, and the more they "discussed" the issue, the sillier it became, and soon these two were laughing at themselves. She was feisty, this woman. And she didn't give an inch. He liked that! Someone that actually stood up to him! And she was intelligent, and finally, he allowed himself to really look at her. The African influence was readily apparent. Combine that with her Spanish ancestry, and her beautiful olive skin, and he could see where this was going. Fast!

Bill and Barb saw it, the instant connection these two had, and excused themselves. So now it was just the two of them, and things began to change. She was smart and beautiful to boot! And she decided that maybe he had been joking after all, and she was attracted to this man. He was charming but polite and caring, and not at all arrogant like he first appeared. They bid each other good night. He to his room; her to her room, and each would think about tonights' encounter and wonder what the hell just happened.

And a lot had happened. Way beyond either of their compre-hension. These two would be joined together in ways neither could have imagined after their first encounter.

What a great time Bocas offered up! They would ride the waves off Red Frog beach over and over again, these would be body surfers. The waves would spit them out over and over again, yet they would not give way. On occasion, they caught a wave, and the next fifty failures meant nothing!

He would meet her after her shift each night and they would talk the night away. They grew close, fast, and he started to wonder if she was the one. The one who could settle him down. He and Maria had come so close, in fact, he was sure they would have had a good chance . . . but . . . it was not to be. Angelina didn't have a chance, not because she wasn't right, but paranoia and fear would not allow him to even take the chance. He missed her, but . . . it was too late.

How could he even think this way about Karena; they had only met days before? Yet, he felt free, and whatever had haunted him was now long gone, he was sure of that. But, he shouldn't have been. He was putting her in a situation unbeknownst to him, that had danger written all over it!

15.

I AM THE ONE

She thought of this man as she worked. Why him? Why had she fallen for him so quickly. And he seemed to have fallen for her as well. As if her life wasn't complicated enough already. But, if he felt like she did, then she was going for it, damn the consequences! When she spotted his notebook, she put pen to paper and started to write. She caught herself fantasizing about the future, their future! Crazy! She couldn't help herself and she wrote these words, words that still resonate today: I AM THE ONE!

And he thought of her. He wondered if she thought of him the same way. It happened so fast, and yet, it seemed so right. And, so wrong! So? If she felt the same way, then he was going for it. Consequences be damned! She had written in his book, and when he found what she had written, he was confused. For she had written words that he cherished still today: I AM THE ONE!

Bill and Barb had decided they needed to move on. This friend of theirs had better come with them. Did he not understand the danger he was in? They'd been talking to a few of the locals and what they'd heard did not bode well for their friend!

So they invited him out for dinner that evening at the Riptide. The best fish and chips in the land, according to those in the know.

Dinner on a boat is, well, just cool. Simple as that. The food is good! The beer is even better! They needed to talk to him. Now.

They knew he could be stubborn. He seemed to thrive on risk. Those two were tight, real tight, and it was obvious to everyone around them. He'd seen this man in action earlier, but this was different. They knew what the answer would be. But, they had to try.

Aaron listened politely. He agreed with their logic. But, he had to remind them that many months ago, when he had started this journey, he had made a pact with himself. That pact was pretty simple: trust your gut, or that small voice, or whatever you want to call it, and he did. Doors opened for him time and time again. Dozens of times. Coincidences? Forget it! His gut told him to stay. He made a decision. He would drop his anchor in troubled waters and ride out the inevitable storm! As if that would surprise anyone!

The "followers" knew that the couple had left, and they knew that he had stayed. That's all they cared about. No need to keep too close to him,; as long as he was in the country, Marcos was happy. He didn't need this gringo just yet, but when he did, he wanted him close by.

So Bill and Barb were back on the road. As much as they had enjoyed this snapshot of Panama, they were eager to get back to Costa Rica. Maybe it was just them, but they sure felt a lot safer once they crossed that border. They would miss their friend, but they had promised to keep in touch. Hopefully he would be around to keep in touch with! He would miss them as well. He and Bill had become good friends, and he would definitely miss him. He finally had someone he could actually talk to and now he was alone again.

Red Frog was too isolated, too lonely for him. So he headed into Bocas. At least there were people around. She was working most of the time. So he found a condo and settled in. They got to know each other. Well. They knew that their love would find a way. They knew it would be difficult and they knew it would be complicated. More complicated than he could ever have imagined.

16.

BOCAS DEL TORO

Bocas is in its' own little world. Separated from most of reality as we know it. Charming to some, seedy and dirty, unquestionably, a hangout for many gringos escaping from their own dismal worlds. Here they can be king for a day, and take advantage of the all too willing locals who congregate in such places. Not all gringos are like that, of course, but the local drinking establishments stand testament to the aforementioned. Many stories come out of this area, mostly the unsavoury kind. It seems that not only tourists frequent this area, but "others," who seem to pass through with a somewhat different agenda, perhaps staying one step ahead of their pursuers. Then there are the "strangers" who are obviously up to no good. Some of them come and stay. They never become part of anything. Yet when they come, it has been said, that several locals over the years have disappeared, to put it politely, and the "strangers" have inherited their properties. No one dare ask, and few dare tell. Or, at least that's how our man heard it.

He stayed around for quite a while, this man. He stuck to himself, friendly but distant. At first they thought he was a tourist, but tourists don't stay that long. Yet he wasn't really a "stranger," in fact, he became well known among the locals. He just "was," whatever that meant.

For a time he felt free. He no longer felt that he was being watched all the time. But he was wrong. He was being watched, but by others, and probably because of his involvement with Karena. She didn't seem overly concerned as long as they observed the "rules" that they had put in place for themselves. Their meetings were clandestine, to be sure. But other than that, all seemed to go quite well.

This little piece of paradise served him well those months. He spent lots of time on or in the ocean and became quite adept at knowing the best spots to dive or snorkel or fish or sight see and all the rest. It seemed strange advising the tourists or travellers who came his way about where they should go, or what they shouldn't miss, and so on. In many ways he thought he had become a local. But he hadn't, and he never would as far as most Panamanians were concerned!

17.

GOODBYE KARENA

Though he and Karena continued on as they were, he was becoming restless and knew he had to return home for a time. He had to get away from here, from her, to get a different perspective on this whole situation. She knew it as well, and even though she didn't want him to go, she knew it was best. With each passing day, she knew that she was jeopardizing her own situation which she had been working on for a whole year prior to meeting him. When they became close, she became worried, but she was afraid of losing him so they kept meeting anyway. She knew what a price she would pay if they were ever caught. And she knew it was best he go.

He told her that he loved her and that he would be back. She told him that she loved him also, and that she would wait. Neither knew for sure whether this was just the stuff of fantasy or whether the love they had professed so soon and so vividly was real. It had happened so quickly, and intensely. It was, in her words, serious right from the start. She had recently come out of a difficult situation and had no energy to invest in a relationship of any kind. She was overloaded before he came on the scene. But he was different, so different. She found she could relax around this man. In fact, she could be utterly vulnerable and that scared her. She had even broken down and cried in front of him! She didn't cry. She was the one that had to keep it together for everyone else. She could not be weak! And yet with him, it was ok. He would never take advantage of her. She had known him for such a short while, but she felt she had known him forever.

He wasn't even sure why he was leaving. The few who had grown aware of his "other" life pleaded with him to stay. They had never met her, and he had made sure of that, but they knew there was a great love affair going on. "How can you leave her?" Michelle could not understand.

"You have found someone you truly love, and who loves you and now you're leaving? Don't go, please!" On one level, he agreed with her. He knew that when he walked away, it may be the last time he ever saw her. But, he didn't think so. They both needed this, and right or wrong, he was going. And so he bid Bocas and the scores of friends he had made, adios.

But he and Karena were not done yet. They jetted off to Panama City and spent a few days away from prying eyes, at least as far as they knew. They enjoyed each other's company as never before and then it was time. And it was difficult. They went to the airport and she got on one plane and he on another, and they flew away to different destinations. Each wondered if they would ever see the other again. They would, but neither knew that at the time!

18.

ALLOWED TO LEAVE?

He had been allowed to leave Panama? How could this be? They had spent months tracking and manipulating this man just to get him into Panama and now the boss was letting him leave?

This made no sense! But, of course it did. To the "puppet master" it made all the sense in the world. They had become close, these two. The deal Marcos had made with Aaron would ensure that the Canuck would be coming back. It didn't hurt one bit that he was involved with one of the locals. He's mine! This Canuck was definitely the real deal. It didn't seem to matter who he came into contact with, gringo or otherwise, people liked this guy. It would take a while to get him fully on board, but one way or the other, he would get him!

Marcos was no fool. He knew exactly what he was doing and why. And although there may have been some risk in letting him go back to Canada for a time, he was willing to risk it. Better to have this man in the country voluntarily. It would certainly be easier to control the situation when they got closer to ground zero.

Marcos had waited countless years to re-emerge; and the time was nearly right. They may have chased him out of his country once before, but now, it would be his turn. He knew how to bring it about.

This government was way too friendly with the foreigners. At the expense of their own people. The people weren't going to take it anymore and he would take advantage of that. So what if he used a few people to achieve his end goal. Sacrifice a few to save a lot. What's wrong with that? If anyone knew what needed to be done, it was him. This country was being run like it belonged to them, not the Panamanians. All this big talk about being pro-business was a bunch of bunk. Why not give away the whole country? Certainly had a good start, this government!

Why wouldn't the foreigners line up at the trough? It was easy pickings aided and abetted by the very protectors of our country! No more! Not if he had his way. And the natives were restless and he could use that to advantage.

The Canadian mining companies would be his "soft" target. Canada, this squeaky clean nation could do no wrong. Bull! They were just like the rest. Take! And take some more! And give only when they needed to "buy" favour or appease a certain group. Well, before long, the world would view them through different eyes, and the government of the day would be forced to reveal its true colours for all to see. This Canuck would be integral in bringing them to their knees.

He was Canadian, he was non military, he fit in perfectly everywhere, and he bore no tie to him.

None! Now, his "friend" would not have appreciated knowing that he was about to help take down a government. But war is war, and they were at war. Only, they didn't know it. He had specific tasks for him, and although not a professional, he would be more than capable of taking care of the "problems." This would take months to achieve, but he was a patient man. After all, he had already waited over 20 years. Another few months, a year at best, and it would all be over.

Then he would emerge from the shadows, and Panama would rise from the ashes once again.

Some though him mad, perhaps insane. " I AM THE ONE! I know what Panama needs, and it's me!" They knew he was powerful, and relentless. They knew he had once held a position of power so knew its' taste. He was not taken lightly. When he spoke it was best that one listen.

With him there was no middle ground. You were either with him, or you were an enemy. Simple as that! Choices would soon have to be made. Either way, heads were going to roll. Pick your side wisely!

But why involve, in fact, hand pick this Canuck? Who was he that he was so special? It made no sense. But Marcos was in charge. It made sense to him. And that was that!

19.

THIS IS YOUR HOME

So he was back in Canada, and wondering why. He didn't have to leave but it seemed to be the right thing to do. Karena had issues that would be a lot easier to deal with when he wasn't around. He knew that. It certainly wouldn't hurt him to get a different perspective on what had taken place these past few months. Besides, he would be heading back to Panama in a couple of months anyway.

He and Marcos had certainly hit it off! And Marcos had offered him an interesting business proposition that he just couldn't ignore. And besides, she was there, and he suddenly had a whole lot more incentive!

They had talked plenty, he and Marcos, over the past months. When Marcos offered to fly him back here in a couple of months on his dime, well, the deal was sealed. He had been interested in doing business here before, but now , it was a given. Perhaps this relationship with Karena had a chance after all. Give it a couple of months apart, and see what happens then.

Life was good! Opportunities were presenting themselves! Good, solid contacts were being established. He was a lucky man and he knew it! Marcos had asked him to keep their involvement on the down low, and, if he didn't mind, leave Karena out of the loop for the time being. At least until they knew where this was all going. Fair enough.

Home welcomed this consummate traveller back into their midst. When he left they knew not when he would return. Perhaps a few months; perhaps a year. They didn't know. He didn't know.

Yet here he was, and they were glad. He was a good friend, the kind of friend you want. Non judgmental, accepting of others idiosyncrasies, and the kind of guy you can tell your "secrets" to. So he kept busy while home. Not a day would go by that he wasn't spending time with family or friends. And of course, spending time at the local McDonalds (he was also a connoisseur of fine food). All too quickly the time would pass and he would feel the need to move on. Panama had grabbed this man in more than one way, and he was anxious to see where this was all going. He had spoken to Marcos on several occasions since he had come home, and it was obvious that he was anxious to get going on some of these projects they had discussed. And he was anxious to see Karena. They had talked daily since he had come home but still, he wasn't sure what to expect. He was anxious to find out. No doubt she was as well!

His family and friends would talk about this man. They would question his kids. Maybe they could talk some sense into him. His home was here. His family was here. What the devil was he thinking? He had let it slip that he was "involved." That was a mistake. Big surprise to them! Him involved? Really! And what they had heard made them uneasy. They knew without him saying a word that this was a dangerous place. Knowing him, he would be in the middle of it! But of course, he downplayed their concerns. He reminded them that he did keep in touch regularly so that they would always know what he was up to. Right! He blogged alright, but what concerned them was not what he wrote, it was the "stuff" between the lines that concerned them. His daughter would define it as "cryptic." She was right, and it was on purpose. One day he would do "something" with those blogs. But for now, he just wanted to keep them interesting and keep his followers entertained. He didn't want them thinking too much about what he was actually up to. Keep it light, and keep it simple, was the intent and he planned on keeping it that way.

20.

BACK TO PANAMA

Karena met him in Panama City. Any doubt either of them had, vanished instantly. Now what?

There were still unresolved issues at play here, and they weren't going away quickly or quietly.

So once again their very existence would, by necessity, be on the down low. This could go on for months. Their love would be tested severely. She would question this man time and again about why he stayed with her. This was her battle, not his, and yet he stood by her. His life would be so much simpler without her in it, and she would not blame him if he walked away. Yet, she prayed he wouldn't, and he didn't.

She had her issues, no doubt about it. He could have got "involved" any number of times down here if that had been his intent. But it never was his intent. It fact, it was his intent NOT to get involved with anybody. Then he met her and his whole world changed. Now they were joined, these two. The devil himself would not come between them (but try he would). Tested they would be. As the situation revealed itself, its complexity increased. Yet he stayed by her side and he would not leave. And she believed him. She loved this "crazy" man. Thank God he had come into her life.

Had she known the future she would have ran screaming in the other direction. For as screwed up as her situation was, it was a cake walk compared to his. But she didn't know that. Neither did he.

But now he was back in Panama and Marcos wanted to meet. It was time for her to leave anyway. So once again they parted, but this was different. Instead of being thousands of miles apart, they were just a few hundred, and they would definitely be staying in touch! If some of these business deals that Marcos had talked about materialized, he would definitely be staying in Panama, and once her situation cleared up, they would begin their life together. Sooner the better as far as he was concerned! And wouldn't that make his family happy! And hers!

He had to admit that his family had legitimate concerns. His "record" with the ladies wasn't exactly stellar. Ironically, their concern wasn't so much for him but for whomever he got involved with. "Don't you dare hurt her! We know you. As soon as the excitement wears off, or you've won, you get bored. Then you move on, and that's not fair." They actually thought they knew him. He had to admit that there was some truth in what they said, but for the most part, he was not the person they thought they knew. As time and distance separated them, they grew to know him even less. He had fled the proverbial nest, and they feared he might not find his way home.

Turns out they were right. They never heard from him again. For a long, long time!

Marcos was well connected and soon Aaron found himself hobnobbing among the chosen few.

He connected well, this man, and soon became well known among Marcos' friends and associates. Yep, he was fitting in brilliantly and would be the perfect "mark" when the time came.

Karena wondered about her man. He was different somehow. A little cocky, arrogant even, and that was not the man she had fallen in love with. Plus, he threw money around indiscriminately, and that she could not tolerate. She saw him less and less. He was always busy. And at the constant beck and call of Marcos! She hadn't even met this man, but she knew she didn't like him. She feared for her man, and she feared for their relationship. He would belittle her fears.

After all, he was making good money which certainly made their life easier, and he was getting connected with the who's who of the business world. If they have to make a living anyway, then why not make a good living? But she knew something was terribly wrong. He should have known. But he didn't. And Marcos smiled.

21.

A LONG, LONG TIME AGO

Aaron had grown up a small town boy. Went to a small town school. Had he followed the path laid out for him, he would have went off to college or university, got a degree, came back to this or some other small town, and taught at the local high school. But Aaron had always been different. The open road called him. It caused his family endless grief. And it was embarrassing.

While the rest of his class mates were building careers and starting families, he was dreaming of tall ships and mountain peaks. He would dream aloud, and others would come along side.

They wanted to share his great adventure. But he soon found that talk was just that: talk. Talk but no action. If it was going to happen, he would be doing it alone. Or, not at all. So, he left. His mother cried, and his dad was angry, and the towns' people shook their collective heads.

It would not be easy, this path he had chosen. He would experience loneliness as never before.

He knew he could return home, eat a little humble pie, and settle back into their life. At least in the early years he could have. But too much time had passed and he couldn't go home. But still he did. For a season.

He dropped in on occasion. Spent time with family and friends. Exchanged stories. And moved on. He no longer fit. He knew it. And they knew it.

This small town boy had travelled extensively, and had certainly gotten himself into a few awkward situations from time to time. But he had the gift of gab, and that would save his hide on more than one occasion. And lead him into a whole lot of situations that would have been better left alone.

If he could have only learned to leave the ladies alone! But that was nearly impossible for our hero. He loved them and they loved him, and their men didn't. So he had left many a town under rather hurried conditions. He didn't go back. And that was a wise decision.

Then he met Celina. Well, actually he and a few of his buddies all saw her at the same time.

And they all fell instantly in love. They acted as most young men act . . . like a bunch of idiots.

But not him. He played it cool. He separated himself from his buddies. He didn't like traveling in packs. He was a loner and he was determined to be alone with her. And it worked. Too well and too quickly. And suddenly he found himself married. Just like that. And in a small town. He had come full circle in spite of himself. Now there were kids, and responsibilities, and his dreams began to fade.

Lest anyone think differently, he loved his kids, and he loved his wife. But she had changed.

Dramatically. He dreaded coming home. This beautiful princess had become the wicked witch.

It was his fault. At least that's what she told everyone. He thought that maybe she was right.

Perhaps if he tried harder or spent more time with the kids, or . . . then one day, he left. He just up and left. With his kids' blessings." Don't stay with her. We'll be ok. She's different when you're not around." That's just the way it was. Turns out that most everyone who knew them were surprised that he'd stayed that long. "Just too bad the kids weren't with you!" But they knew their Mom needed them and they weren't going to leave her. She was great at being a "victim." Soon everyone began avoiding her. And soon her kids could take it no more. She found herself alone.

And she wondered why. She should have known, but she didn't. Besides, she was good at what she did. Hell, she'd been a victim all her life. Everyone else moved on.

The beautiful princess was no longer. In her place stood another. And that's where she stayed.

The kids grew up and found their way. They and their Dad came together again, and they agreed to move forward. As time passed, these three would become close; closer than they had ever been. And she sat alone in her dark, dreary castle, cursing everyone who went by, but especially this man. It was all his fault! Why couldn't they see that!

22.

BUT THAT WAS THEN AND THIS IS NOW

Aaron always called. And then one day he didn't. So Karena called. He liked to tell her how much he loved her. And she liked to hear it. She wasn't as given to words as he was, but she loved this man like no other before. But no answer. She knew in her gut that something was wrong. And she was right.

There was no answer the next day. Or the next. She became very afraid. That is not like him.

Never. So she called around and no one knew or heard anything. She knew he was gone. Just gone. She knew he would never leave her like this. And she was scared. Should she call his kids? She didn't want to alarm them but she knew she had to tell them something, and besides, she had promised them that she would take good care of their Dad!

Three more days would pass without a word so she called and they knew instantly that something was wrong. They had met Karena on a couple of occasions, and as long as their dad was happy, they were happy. They knew she wouldn't be calling just to call. That wasn't their relationship. Then she told them. And their worst nightmares came true! They had always feared for his safety, but he had appeased them in his inimitable way. They knew that whether they protested or not, he would have his way. Now he had disappeared. Even Karena was afraid.

They promised to keep in touch. She would contact the authorities and follow the leads wherever they took her. She would find him for her and for them. When she hung up the phone she burst into tears.

But there was nothing. No news. Nothing. Like he had never even existed! Then she did what she had vowed never to do again: she reached back into her past. If he was alive, they would know! It had been 10 years since she had walked away from that life. My God! Now she needed them desperately. Anything that went down in Panama they would know about. So she reached out. And contact was made. She was picked up late one night, a bag placed over her head and driven to a remote section of town. "God, please protect me. I'm so scared!"

Karena had grown up poor but proud. She was the "princess" In the family. But life was hard and escape became the goal. And when she fell for the wrong guy, it would be all downhill from there.

Her family mourned, for though they had little, they did indeed have love and respect and a sense of belonging.

But she was headstrong and determined to find her way and the promise of a good life was irresistible. It was good at first, even great. But it was not destined to stay that way. She knew not what her husband was "in to" but she would soon find out. She would be the one that paid. And paid dearly! He would walk away scott free. Her family would curse the very ground he walked on and they would mount a full rescue mission to save their "princess" from those who would persecute her.

They disliked the Americans who would lord over them and their country, and Karena had fallen head over heals for a "gringo" and now, everything they had felt for the Americans was proving to be absolutely true!

When the authorities showed up and seized their "books" she knew that something was definitely amiss. When they came after her personally, for after all, was she not the bookkeeper, the truth would be revealed, and she would be hung out to dry! He had money and she didn't, and influence is most often financed by the deepness of ones' pockets.

The truth would come out eventually, but not before she was cast into hell. The women's prison became her home for eight months, and had it not been for for some exceptional friends who could not let this pass, she would probably still be there today.

But she is a fighter, and justice would one day be served. Public apologies would follow but not before it nearly destroyed her life. She would emerge from hell triumphant but bitter and determined to fight the very system that ultimately was forced to free her. It only got worse from there and soon her family were fully engaged in the underground movement.

She had watched her brother die at the hands of the police years ago; beaten to a pulp, and then shot point blank. She had been forced to watch, and left alive as a warning to others who would dare defy them. But all that did was make her even angrier and determined to avenge her brothers' death. So the underground became her home, and she became a warrior within the movement. She had always believed in their cause. And she believed in her people. But the government of the day was no friend of hers, or of anybody, for that matter, unless you were one of the chosen few. They couldn't seem to understand that the freedom fighters were working for the good of all the people, not just some of the people. We are not your enemy. But, they were still hunted down and shot like dogs in the street. When her brother fell, she picked up a weapon and never looked back. For a long, long time. She did what she had to do and took her place among the freedom fighters of that time. Then one day she had enough. She quit and went home to raise her children. She supported the movement, and does so to this day. Even as the governments changed, and promises were made, nothing really changed. Corruption ruled and the common man was always the loser. And always would be. But still they fought on, and she prayed that they would help her. "Please help me find my husband. Please!" So she told them her story. They knew of "Marcos" and if Aaron was being held by him or his ilk, this might not end well. There had been rumblings for months, and frankly, for the most part, they liked what they were hearing. But, they would check it out. She was one of them, and her brother had been a leader in the movement, and now, a martyr. "When we know, you'll know. Don't contact us again. You're putting us at risk."

As the days passed into weeks and the weeks into months, she began to lose hope. She loved him so, and they had been through so much. It could not end this way! But it did end that way. She went back to her home and she cared for her kids as never before. But each month, there was money deposited into her account. The account they had jointly set up so long ago. He had set up an auto transfer to ensure that even if he was out of the country, they would always be ok. But for how long? If he was putting money into the account, then why wasn't he in contact with her? Or was this some cruel hoax designed to send a message. If so, what? Leave it alone or the money stops! Or, perhaps a payout into his account for who knows what. But it gave her hope. Not a lot, but a little hope was better than none. So she resolved to stay the course. And she did. For a very long time. But finally, the floodgates broke, and when she arose, she knew what she had to do. And no thanks to the freedom fighters! No, none at all! But what she didn't know was that many of them had become sympathizers and supported Marcos, and indeed, they knew of Aaron. He was one of them. And they weren't about to tell her.

23.

I OWN YOU NOW . . .

Aaron was confused and alone. And stuck in some seedy hotel. And badly beaten. When he tried the door, it was locked. What the hell? So would begin the assault on this man.

They owned him now, and he would "disappear" from this point on. Oh yes, his people would try and find him. But a few bucks here and there would ensure that he wouldn't be found, at least not until they wanted him found.

They knew about her, but she was no concern. She would forget about him; he was just another gringo taking advantage of the locals. She would get on with her life. That's what they do around here. What choice? Not like she could afford to hire investigators. If she was foolish enough to pursue this, well, she'd be dealt with. And it wouldn't end well for her.

Each day they would visit him. And indoctrinate him. And beat him. Soon he became passive and compliant. The drugs began to do their job and he slowly began to lose himself. They knew what they were doing, these people. It wasn't the first time they had been called to "fix" a problem.

They began to test him. Small assignments at first. Just to see how he handled himself. They knew he could charm his way into a situation but did he have the jam to carry out the assignment and disappear into the wood work as if he'd never even been there? So they did their rounds. They hob knobbed with their "mark." Another good old boy from the US who thought he was a big shot, especially down here. Well, fine. Play along, set him up and take him down without him even realizing it. Always take advantage of their greed . If there was one thing that they knew for sure, it was that they were all flipping greedy! That's where he would come in. Schmooze with the enemy. Make him like you, and trust you. After you've robbed him blind, he'll come to you looking for a shoulder to cry on. And never be the wiser. In fact, they would commiserate together because they had both been fleeced, both taken by some unscrupulous low life. Of course they couldn't report it to the authorities since this deal was, well, off the books so to speak. They would go their own way, these two. One would be congratulated on a job well done. He would be locked down, as usual, but there would be no beating this night.

This would continue in the weeks and months to come. The "marks" would, by design, be more and more sophisticated and higher up the food chain. He proved to be incredibly adaptable, and it mattered not with whom or where he was, he could fit in easily. Without question.

He began to enjoy his role. He was good at it and no "mark" was too big for him to tackle.

But he knew something was off. He lived in a perpetual fog. Thank God for the drugs. Kept the edge off. Kept him focused. He was a soldier and he would do his duty. Still, he kept having flashbacks. There were faceless people reaching out to him. Not in a bad way. More in an embracing way. He wished he knew what that was all about. But he took pride in his role and would not let Marcos down.

Marcos was pleased with this gringo. Not only was he proving to be an incredible soldier, but he seemed to have completely forgotten his previous life. Strange. They knew they could turn him, but even they were surprised at how quickly he had acquiesced. Not only had he come on side but he was committed to their cause, and that was a definite bonus. A few more successful assignments and they would be ready. Then all hell would break loose! He had waited for years to get to this place and this time, and he would not be denied. So close! Be patient. Just a little longer.

But Aaron had remembered something. Vaguely. He tried mightily to remember but he couldn't. But he wouldn't quit. He knew he couldn't tell them. Yet he served them and would continue to do so, but he knew something was off. Slowly but surely he would find out. But right now, he needed a hit.

How was it possible to control this man so easily? In a word: scopolamine, better known as Devil's Breathe. It was unpredictable but extremely effective and in him it found the perfect ally. He had always been a different sort, had always marched to the beat of his own drummer. Definitely not compliant and yet here he was. Almost robotic, and yet, when required, he could turn on the charm and fit into any situation. Even they were confused and they were not easily fooled. He was no fool either but he knew he was strung out and he knew he was dangerously close to slipping into the abyss. He knew he was being manipulated but he seemed unable to grasp its full context. He had a real life somewhere, and yet it too escaped his grasp. He tried valiantly to hang on to whatever semblance of reality he could.

Psychologists would have a field day with him, no question about it. Devil's Breathe? Please! But they would be wrong! He knew not where to turn. Names and faces escaped him, that is, until they needed him for an assignment. And then, as if flicking a switch, he was there, fully. This independent man had become fully dependent on them. And that was the way they wanted it.

It was time to switch it up. Marcos felt that he was ready. If they were ever going to pull this off, the time was now. And so he went over his plan. Time and time again. He had invested years to get to this point. This gringo was perfect, and expendable if things went sideways. His people, including her, had finally given up, and were convinced that he lie dead somewhere yet undiscovered. Perfect.

His country had been raped and pillaged by foreigners for far, far too long with the consent of the government, which treated the outsiders better than they had ever treated their own people. He knew this wouldn't change overnight but once it got rolling, it would be nearly impossible to stop. His influence dated back to the time of Noriega. He had stood tall and dared to defy the government of the day. And nearly lost his life. He became a symbol to those freedom fighters back then, and he still held sway even to this day. Even though Panama had overthrown Noriega and embraced democracy, corruption continued to rear its ugly head time and time again. And though the time of the freedom fighters should have long since passed, it didn't, and still flourishes to this day. Albeit, underground.

24.

THE INDIGENOUS OF PANAMA

There are almost 300,000 indigenous in Panama. They're being pushed to the brink by foreigners and by their own government. And they're mad as hell. They are beginning to organize and that does not bode well for the powers that be.

They have cause for concern. The constitution is supposed to protect them. It doesn't. Plain and simple. So, the foreigners come with outstretched arms and they are warmly greeted, and once again, the Panamanian people suffer. But on the world stage the word is out: Panama is open for business! We will give you anything you want! And quit reading all that crap on the Internet. Come one, come all!

And they came, and they come, and Canada is well represented. Way less attention down here, and certainly more profitable. They know mining, these Canadians. And so few restrictions! The indigenous? Let the government take care of that "problem." Canada was just part of the problem but because it is so docile, Marcos felt it was the perfect place to begin. They wouldn't know what hit them! Then the world would have to take note. Panama would truly emerge as the great nation it was meant to be! And Marcos would be its saviour!

He had tapped into this discontent years ago. In fact, this would be his vehicle to achieve his end goal. It would be legitimate, mostly. This was a powder keg and if a few of their own people got hurt in the process, it was still a small price to pay to save their country from the foreigners!

Over 20% of Panama is occupied by legally constituted indigenous territories or comarcas. At one time there were over 60 tribes but that has been reduced to 7 or so, with the Ngobe-Bugle representing over 60% of the indigenous population. The Kuna tribe accounts for about 16% or so, even though they are the best known. The rest make up the balance.

The Kunas have been leaders in the fight for indigenous rights. They were the first to establish comarcas in Panama, and have served as an example to the other tribes, especially the Ngobe-Bugle which are becoming incredibly active in the fight for the right to exist on their own, legally constituted lands. The tribes are becoming more and more united and better organized and are able to put up a united front against their oppressors, and would be exploiters. That is causing grief for a nation that likes to pat its own back at the expense of its own people. Marcos would use this. He was a brilliant man, perhaps too smart for his own good. And what one had intended for good, could lead to disastrous consequences. But no one dared challenge this man and he would have his way. So, stir he would. Why not take a volatile situation and add a touch of fuel to the fire?

The Tribes had fought many a battle to preserve as best they could the lands they occupied. Now the government was ignoring these treaties, or ripping them up or threatening their very existence. All in the name of progress. The government would take help from whoever offered it. An exchange, if you will. Your technology, your expertise. We will roll out the red carpet. So what if it is stained with the blood of our own people, especially the indigenous! We can beat silence into them. We know how to keep them quiet.

Or so they thought. And they did so for a time. But that time has passed and they can be silenced no more. So they rise up. As an indigenous nation. Silent. We cannot fight you with weapons, but we can fight you with words, and with numbers.

So they protest, and they block highways and byways, borders and airports. Silently. And this gets attention. For it takes not long in a country such as Panama to suffer greatly. Fuel in a place such as this runs out quickly. Merchants are unable to get to their markets. And tourists, the almighty tourists, are inconvenienced.

They are vocal, and they go viral. The world watches. Some will come on side. Some will cancel their travel plans and go to someplace "safer." The business community will take a second look. They will weigh it out. Risk versus reward. How can we exploit, oh sorry, how can we become a player in an emerging market, and still retain our squeaky clean image abroad? Remember, it's all about image. We need to at least appear to be doing the right thing. After all, aren't we, as a responsible company, merely looking to create a win-win scenario.? Why can't we be leaders in bringing this country into the light? First World they want to be, and since we have all the answers, we have a duty and a responsibility to assist them in this endeavour. If we make a few profits along the way, well, it is free enterprise, isn't it? This is a democracy, is it not? So it goes. And they come. This certainly does not apply to everyone, lest this be taken that way. Not at all.

But, being a do good society first and foremost, the mining companies would naturally want to come into the indigenous lands and help them develop their communities. So, in come the NGOs/charities with nothing but good intentions and people dedicated to helping the indigenous. And that is great. Except that there is an underlying motive. Simply put, we will do this in exchange for the extraction companies being allowed on your lands. See. Very simple, really. That is how it works. And has worked in many other have not nations throughout the world. Many of these companies' treatment of the "people" has been less than stellar. But, as long as shareholders are happy . . .

25.

THE GOVERNMENT

President Fernando Hernandez, a self-made millionaire, has orchestrated an incredible PR campaign designed to bring investment into Panama in a big way. There is nothing wrong with that. In fact, it would be good for the economy of Panama, thus the people. All the people, right? Maybe not. Maybe just some of the people. The "haves" definitely, and the foreigners, for sure. The rich get richer and the poor, well, who cares. Or so it seems.

But the indigenous are growing bolder. Leaders are emerging and the world is watching. The world is putting names and faces together. The people refuse to stay in the shadows any longer. That is problematic for the government, which is unable to still that silent voice that has suddenly become a roar.

Various laws were written into existence in the Mining Code to offer protection of sorts to the peoples of these lands. It was not perfect but it was a beginning. Though bribery and corruption ruled the day, it was a start. Then Hernandez began changing laws at will; stripping away what basic rights the indigenous had, and the war was on.

The indigenous would be silent no longer. They came from the highlands and they came from the lowlands; they came from near and far. They erected their roadblocks. The Pan American highway would once again be victimized, and so would community after community throughout the land. The borders would not be granted relief in the hours and days to come. The tourists, well, they would tell their stories, in real time, and the world would watch.

The government would acquiesce. For a time the indigenous would take down their road blocks and return to their homes. But, they were becoming better and better organized. They now had the worlds' attention. As good as the governments PR machine was, and is, they were finding their voice and staring down what was once invincible.

How Marcos delighted in this. The hated government brought to its knees! Taken on by the poorest of the poor. With over 40% of the population living in abject poverty, and a government run by the super-rich, it was inevitable that the rich would want to get richer. That's the way it is, and that's the way it's always been. But of course, the poor would benefit, wouldn't they? Perhaps one needs look at the surrounding countries that have had the "privilege" of giving away their resources to the outsiders. That is why there are so many "First World Countries" down there. That certainly worked, didn't it? Yes, Marcos was a happy man. The country was in disarray, the government was shaken, others were doing his dirty work for him, and he still had a couple of cards up his sleeve. And that is where his new found " friend" would come in. Besides, he was expendable. He would ensure that he could never be traced back to him. All was well in the world of this would be king. For now.

Aaron partied long and hard with these new friends. Canadians they were, and it had been a long time since he had spent any time with anybody from Canada. They were down here at the invitation of the government, and how sweet it was. These were mining experts and their assignment was simple: make us money. Lots of it! If they were to get their hands dirty, it certainly wouldn't be in the mines. That's why we have the locals. Put them to work. Don't worry about the working conditions. Worry about the shareholders. That's the important thing. There are plenty of other ways to get your hands dirty down here. Whether naive or otherwise, they liked to talk. And talk they did, and with every scoop full, they ensured their eventual burial. He took it all in. He commiserated when appropriate, and he applauded at the appropriate time. They liked this guy. It was great to have a fellow Canuck to hang out with.

And this Canuck brought along his own spade. Since they were doing so well at digging holes, he might as well join them. When the time was right, he would cross over to the other side. But they wouldn't know, and they wouldn't find out.

He would have little sympathy for them. In fact, he was embarrassed that his country had so little regard for the rights of the people. How did they put it: "It's not our problem."

Had he known that he was merely a pawn in Marcos' game, he would have fled then and there. But instead, he looked up to this man whose only agenda was to give his people a voice. Yes, he was drawing outside the lines a little, but his intentions were honourable. Had he only known! But he didn't. When he looked back on this time in his life, he was staggered by how gullible he had been. But hind sight only comes later, and this was now.

26.

WE HAVE NAMES AND FACES TOO

Her name was Silvia Carrera, and she had been elected chief or general cacique of the tribe. She was not afraid. Nor were her people. And they respected her. She was a woman of peace. She was a woman to be reckoned with. But her weapon was words. Mere words. Except mere, they were not. Under her watch, the world would see what they saw daily. She held in her hands, for all to see, spent riot equipment used against them in earlier peaceful protests. Let's see: rubber bullet casings, shotgun shells, sting ball grenades, tear gas canisters and the like. And photos of the recently killed, and the names of the wounded in previous "peaceful" demonstrations. Again the world watched. The government conspired. And were outraged. They invited her to the palace. But she would not go. The tension mounted. The foreigners were becoming uneasy. Panama: open for business! Really? But there was money to be made here, so let's stay awhile and see how this plays out. Besides, they will offer us even more incentives to stay!

His name was Jose Carranza. He was 14 when a bullet ripped through his skull killing him instantly. In front of his Mother and little brother. They had walked for miles to join the protests. Now he lay dead. They would say he had tried to attack an officer, and was shot in self defence. Like they always said. Immediately go on the offensive. Deny any culpability, regardless of the evidence. And get your PR machine working.

But this wasn't going away. This wasn't the first death by cop, and it wouldn't be the last, but it would ignite a nation. And it would draw the attention of the world.

Spin as they might, this huge propaganda machine could not stop the suspicion of something gone wrong, something slightly amiss. Outsiders watched and waited.

Blood is not easily washed away. It leaves a stain that cannot be easily removed. The indigenous throughout the land are packing cell phones and recording everything, and have learned that these guns without bullets are far more effective than any loaded weapon could ever be.

But when opportunity arises and money is to be made, free enterprise will always work. Except it's not "free." Rarely is it not off the backs of those least able to defend themselves.

We are complicit in these affairs. Most us are mere shareholders and trust what has been presented to us. We are trying to get ahead. And invest so we can better out lives and the lives of our children. Perfectly admirable. Whatever else is going on is certainly not our fault. Is it?

Aaron was not impressed with what he was seeing and hearing. The more time he spent with these mining execs the more determined he was to bring them down. They cared not one iota about the people, or the environment. What they cared about was profits. That was it. Everything else was nothing more than an irritant. The government had better get those people under control!

27.

WE'RE RIGHT . . . WHAT DO THEY KNOW?

A country suffering the effects of extreme poverty and poor medical care would do well to consider any options that would alleviate the suffering of its people's. There are many wealthy nations ready, willing, and able to assist those in need, especially the really desperate ones. For a desperate nation may well trade away its soul (or resources) if it can be fed today.

Unfortunately, those who will be fed are not necessarily those who are most in need; more than likely, the ones being fed are those most in greed. Of course, a bone will be thrown here and there to keep the great unwashed quiet. It only happens all the time. Choose any country you want, and step back in time to see where the truth lies. And I'm not just talking third world countries.

Cynical? Perhaps. True? Most likely. Does anyone really care? Some do; some would say that they do; some don't, and most just turn the channel. Some of you are definitely channel surfers. After all, that stuff is depressing!

Mario, Elana, and their kids live just downstream from the Canadian Mining Corporation known as Kan Mines Inc. They are

Kunas, proud, independent, hunters and gatherers. With a new neighbour run amok. With the consent of their government. When their kids started acting "different" they grew concerned and sought medical attention. There is a lot of sickness across the land on a regular basis, but the medical community was seeing something a little different here. Respiratory problems, especially in the very young were rampant. Other unusual medical problems were manifesting themselves among the indigenous peoples, especially those in proximity to the numerous mining operations dominating so much of their territories.

Woe to those who would question the possibility of a link of any sort. After all, are we not here as saviours of your country? You should appreciate us and thank us, not spread rumours and embarrass us.

Mario and Elana were not alone. This was happening not only through their tribe, but throughout the other tribes as well. There would be much wailing and gnashing of teeth in the months and years to come. Sickness would become a way of life, and many of their young would not be spared. But still the government would not acknowledge their plight. The investments grew, and the fat became fatter, and they congratulated themselves on a job well done.

We are a first world country they would declare. Check us out. Who could deny that Panama City is a cosmopolitan centre? Just look at our skyline. Anybody who is anybody is here. We are the banking capital of Central America. Corporate giants live among us. But, peer through the looking glass and another portrait begins to emerge. And that is not to their liking. Perhaps all that glitters is not gold, and what gold there is, was bought on the backs of those least able to stand up for their rights. And mothers cry and babies die!

He didn't really know what Marcos intentions were exactly. All he knew for sure was that his job was to get up close and personal with as many of these execs as possible. Blend in, become part of their inner social circle. Not a bad gig. He always had money in his pocket, got to eat and drink at the best places in town, invited to all the best parties. If this was work, then he was all in! Yet, he knew that there was an end game in here somewhere, and he knew that he would figure prominently some way or other. But, Marcos knew what he was doing. When he was called upon, he would answer the bell.

28.

HE BEGINS TO REMEMBER

What a life he was living these days! He could hardly remember what life had been like before he and Marcos got together. Come to think about it, that was kind of weird. He remembered being back in Canada for a spell. And then he had returned to Panama and to . . . Oh my God! What the hell had happened? Karena. He had returned to Karena, and he had went to work for Marcos and then . . . nothing. Karena . . . Karena . . . How could he not remember her? Oh my God! Her name had just popped out of his mouth and now he couldn't let it go. Where was she? Why weren't they together? Why now? This was crazy! Maybe he was crazy! Yet, he knew not to speak of her. He wrote her name down lest he forget it again. He was confused, and suddenly he was lonely. And he began to weep.

He began to remember. A snippet here, a snippet there. None of it made any sense. He knew he was being watched. He knew there was something seriously amiss. He had been devoured by a monster. And he knew not this monsters' name . . . not yet! He should have, and he would. In due course!

Her name began to haunt him. Karena. How was it even possible to forget a whole section of his life like that? The feelings that were beginning to surface were starting to scare him. She wasn't just somebody in his life . . . and he began to choke up. Oh my God! Sleep he would not find in the days to come. He tried so hard to will her to him. Expose yourself to me. Let me see you. Please! But she didn't, and try as he might, he could not cajole her out of the recesses of his mind.

Again, they knew something was amiss. So they watched him. Like a hawk. For a time. Then they didn't. He was a strange duck to begin with. Besides, his wings were already clipped. Not to worry. So, the less they looked at him, the more he looked for her. She was in there somewhere and he was bound and determined to find her. When he did . . . well, actually he wasn't sure what he would do, if she was even real!

But she had to be! These feelings were way too real to not be real. So then why didn't she come to him? Yet he knew that he dares not ask. He began to wonder about Marcos. He took his blinders off. He began to see the world through his own eyes. What he saw today was not what he had seen yesterday. Tomorrow would offer up its' own version of the truth. So he would remain the good soldier, and continue down this path laid out before him. But now he could see, and with each passing day, his vision grew clearer. She began to come into focus. He would call out to her, and reach out to her . . . but she was not there. He would take to his bed each night and he would hold her close, and fall asleep knowing she was by his side. If only.

29.

KARENA . . . IF ONLY

She knew that if he was in Canada he would be doing exactly what she was doing right now. Or, if he was here with her, they would, along with the kids, be listening to the pastor deliver his message. In Spanish. Heck, he spoke almost as good as they did, this blue eyed gringo. He was accepted here. He said he would fit in, and he did. If he was still alive, and she choked back her tears, he would be reaching across time and space to be with them. She sensed his presence. She knew he was out there somewhere. One day . . . She spoke little of him for the pain was too much to bear. Most thought he had deserted her. Just another gringo! Big surprise! But she knew this man, and she knew he would never forsake her. Not him.

So she went through the motions. She was a good mom and she would do her best to raise these children so they would have opportunities that she never had. One day he would come home again and they would once again be a family. But she would never let the kids see her cry. She had to be strong. For her and for them.

She felt guilty. So guilty. She knew his daughters missed him so, and she felt that she was to blame. If not for her . . . they assured her time and again that it was not her fault. He always did whatever he wanted. And he wanted to be with her. They were okay with that.

But still, they missed him and prayed for his return. So they kept in contact with her. They knew that he would contact her, and they knew she would contact them. So every time the phone rang, it was with apprehension mixed with anticipation, and they knew that one day the call would come. How does one prepare for that inevitability? Will it be good news or will their worst nightmares come true?

30.

MARCOS REVEALED

Marcos knew that one day he would have his revenge. They had taken everything away from him so very long ago. Now, he would make them pay! Corruption was long the master negotiator in this country, his country, and it would not go away soon. Fine! Then he would use it as well, and turn the dragon upon itself. It would devour the millionaires club that ruled the land. A class of the privileged few where enough was never enough, and deals with the devil were a daily occurrence.

The indigenous had been pushed too far this time. The government and the foreign intrusion had awakened a sleeping giant that would no longer be put back in its cage. Pushed to the brink they were, again and again, until finally they could take no more.

Sickness, disease, abject poverty, death, and destruction of their ancestral homes would define these people. Illiteracy ran rampant, and their own people would treat them as they would a dog. In a country suffering extreme poverty, those who did sympathize could do little but silently protest, for to be vocal would mean loss of what little privileges they already had. And that is the truth.

Marcos would tap into this discontent and utter abuse of power. He knew how to engage the people, all the people, save for the elitist few.

So, it was time to stir up the masses. And though he would rather have worked his magic from inside the government, that would expose him and he was not ready for that. So instead, it was time to further infiltrate the mining companies, and the best place to start was the Kan Mining Corporation. Besides, his "gringo" was in nice and tight with this group. It was time for him to step up and deliver the goods.

He knew this would be touchy, and that his man would balk at his assignment. But regardless, it was going to happen. Perhaps it was time to remind him that they knew his family well. Those kids sure were cute. And Karena, well, they could get to her any time they wanted.

But, Marcos would have a little chat with him first. He was a good soldier, this man, and perhaps he would go along with the cause. Sure would make it a lot easier. There was a lot to do. This wouldn't be easy , and it would be delicate, but it would work.

Yes, a few of the indigenous would be expendable, but the greater good would be served. Panama would be free of these invaders, and the present government would be taken down. He would be the architect, and if not king, then definitely the king maker.

Aaron knew that Marcos was switching it up and that he had an assignment for him. He knew it was important. He knew it involved his mining buddies and he knew he wasn't going to like it. That much he knew. And he was right.

Aaron was stunned. He wanted to get up and walk away right then and there. I mean, he knew he was to buddy up to those guys, and he wasn't entirely stupid, or was he? What the hell was he thinking?

Then Marcos dropped a bomb shell and everything changed. Suddenly she came into focus . . . and it was real. It was all real. And he wanted to puke. He laid his head on the bar and he cried. There was no relief to be had. He was afraid. Very afraid. He began to remember . . . everything. He knew he had made a deal with Lucifer himself.

31.

I REMEMBER

Karena was no longer a vague memory. Now she was in mortal danger. And she didn't even know it! Because of him. She kept telling him over and over that she didn't trust Marcos, that something was amiss. But he knew better. And then, he had disappeared. Just walked away from her and his life. He didn't even remember doing that. Yet, that's exactly what he did!

He would do what Marcos asked. At least until he figured something out. Now they were watching him like hawks, less he bolt. But he wouldn't. He had no doubt in his mind that they would go after her and the kids. He couldn't even warn her. Hell, if she heard his voice she'd probably freak out. And how could he explain this to her. He couldn't even explain it to himself. But one day he would find a way. But for now, he would be the good soldier and do his masters bidding. But when the time was right . . .

Can Henderson was the Canuck he had grown closest to. They'd shared many a drink these two. And Cam had certainly let him into his world. Two marriages gone wrong, bankrupt once, and hospitalized on one occasion for overdosing on some prescription meds that he had let get the better of him. Finally, he had asked for an overseas assignment to get away from everything and everyone he knew. That had worked for a time, but these past few months had shook him up a lot. He knew that the indigenous were opposed to the mining operations in the area, but he had no idea of what was really taking place. Now he knew. And what he knew turned his stomach. He was a big part of it and he was stuck. In fact, if he and his counterparts were doing in their country what they were doing here, they would be behind bars, no doubt about it!

So he told our man everything. And everything he told him was passed on to Marcos and company. Marcos would build his case, one incriminating statement after the other. None of this would stand up in a court of law, but then, that was never the intention anyway. He would take down these mining companies, and if this was done correctly, the government would soon follow.

So it fell to his "soldier" to gather evidence. And compile evidence, and implicate the other major players. After all, they all hung together socially, and they all liked to talk. He was "in" and just one of the crowd. As he became part of the furniture, their words were no longer guarded, and they dug their holes deeper and deeper.

Ironically enough, he agreed with Marcos that these companies needed to be taken to task. He probably could have been talked into doing this willingly. But now . . . threatening his family, what the hell was up with that? But, he would continue to co-operate and let them think they had him where they wanted him. Truth is, they did.

He desperately wanted to contact her. These past days and nights had overwhelmed him. And he remembered everything. Her, the kids, his kids, his family, everything. None of them knew that he was even alive. He dare not contact anyone. He had no doubt that they would follow through on their threats. Would she ever be able to forgive him? He had deserted her. He may not have known it at the time, but that is exactly what had happened. The Doctors would have a field day with this one. In fact, he wasn't sure he believed it himself! But, he would have never abandoned her. Never! God, I pray she knows that! Please God, that's all I ask!

If Marcos thought he "had" him, well, let him think that. But one day, he would get his. And he would make sure that it was up close and personal. No one would know. Like no one knew what he was up to now. He had been well trained. By Marcos. One day Marcos would find out just how well trained he was!

The "puppet master" was delighted with himself. It was all coming together. His man was proving to be even more than he had expected. Threatening his family, well, that was the icing on the cake, and ensured his loyalty. He had him in his pocket, no doubt about it!

Had he only known, he would have put a bullet through his head right then and there. This wouldn't be the only mistake Marcos would make. Not by a long shot!

Karena continued to work on the house; their house. They had scraped every penny they could together to make it happen. It wasn't much but it was theirs. If only he could see it now. He would be surprised. She knew he wasn't that keen on the idea at first but he had warmed up when he saw how excited she was . This would be their home! She could not hold back the tears. He would not have abandoned them! Not him! Something terrible had happened but she would never, ever give up on him. She knew in her heart of hearts that if he could be here with them, he would be. She knew her family thought she was crazy but too bad! They didn't know him like she did!

His kids kept in touch with her from time to time. But there was so little to say. Every time the phone rang from one or the other, their heart would stop for fear that there may be a message about him that none of them wanted to hear. So they went about their lives. What else was there to do? They knew that one day the call would come and that's when they would deal with it. Whatever it was.

He had always kept in touch with those he held near and dear. That was one thing they could always count on. By phone, email, or in person, he would show up. Guaranteed! If he cared for you or felt you were important in his life, you'd know. He wasn't the "conditional" sort. If you were, he wasn't interested. And now his silence was deafening. And they were afraid.

32.

CAM'S STORY

Cam had worked with the mining corporation for almost 10 years when this assignment presented itself. He was on a down hill spiral. This just might breathe some new life into him. If it didn't . . .

He'd had to adapt when he came down here. Things weren't done like they were back home. What they would be shut down for back home was common practice here. In fact, what they were doing here was downright criminal, regardless of where it was. Waterways were polluted as a matter of course. Just don't talk about it. He had heard the rumours about the sweet heart deals their company and others had made with the powers that be. It sickened him. But, he needed this job, and if he quit now, he would be blackballed or worse.

It wasn't long until he no longer saw what was going on. He certainly wasn't going to open his mouth! Yet, he watched these protests and he knew why they were there. It wasn't his babies who were dying, or his mom who was getting sicker and sicker by the day. He didn't have to worry about what he would eat or where he would live day after day. Like they did.

As much as he tried to pretend it wasn't real, it was, and he knew it. Slowly, whatever principles he once embraced, were set aside. He was now a full blown member of the establishment. Oh yes, he could talk about the benefits for the Panamanian people; how their company was benefiting the country economically, and how they were supporting various groups that were providing much needed medical aid and other support to those most in need. Or, he could have talked about how they were were raping and plundering the most vulnerable in this land. But, he didn't. He wouldn't. And he couldn't. For to do so would reveal his own hypocrisy and how pathetic he had become.

Thank God he had finally found someone to talk to. Someone who wasn't a part of the company. A fellow Canuck that was "safe."

He would tell Aaron everything. This man understood him. They had become fast friends, these two. It wasn't long until he had revealed everything. Everything that had been pent up for so long. It felt good. And it felt right. If there was just something he could do. But, there wasn't.

Cam would soon learn that there was a lot he could do. In fact, there was a lot he had already done. He would be doing a whole lot more in the days ahead. He might even have a chance to redeem his soul.

Slowly the tangled web would envelope this man, and though he knew not, there would be no escape for him. He was "in", like it or not. Another piece of the puzzle was finding its way home. But, for now, enjoy the company of your new found friend. Because, he would be needing a friend in the days to come!

Aaron knew that he would have to convince Cam to do the right thing. Yeah, right! Like he did! What a couple of losers! But, he was good at his job and he would convince him that it could be done and no one would be the wiser.

Cam began to gather the information his friend had requested. Reports and documentation that should never have seen the light of day offered themselves up for his perusal. He knew he was caught. And there was nothing he could do about it. Yet, he knew that what he was doing was the "right" thing to do.

How had he gone so far astray? When he had first joined the company he thought he had hit the jack pot. He was the poster boy and destined for great things. But, he had become arrogant and self serving. He began to believe his own press. So he started "taking" what didn't belong to him. Then one day he took "her." And that would be the beginning of the end. For she "belonged" to none other than Bob Gartly himself, President and CEO of Kan Mining Corporation. And she told.

Strangely enough he wasn't fired on the spot. But, he was demoted time and time again. To make an example, it appeared. His pride accompanied his fall. Then his wife tired of his incessant whining, accompanied by his fits of rage, and booted him to the curb.

Finally, he could take it no more. Either he got the hell out of here or take a long walk on a short plank. Something had to give. And it did. When the opportunity to move to Panama presented itself, he was gone. Out of sight and out of mind. That's the way it stayed until he met Aaron, his new found friend. Now his back was being pushed to the wall. Again! But, for very different reasons. He loathed the fact that he was being forced to do this mans' bidding, yet, in some perverse way, he had bought into it. Should he feel bad? Or guilty? Not a chance!

Too bad he hadn't stood tall way back then. But he hadn't. Well, today he would! They would pay dearly! Maybe Aaron was right. Maybe he could redeem his soul!

Marcos was pleased. His gringo was doing a good job. In fact, a great job. He never mentioned his family. Not even once! Strange. If this kept up they would be ready to deliver the death blow in a matter of months! Then all hell would break loose!

He would have liked to take them all down at the same time but the risk of being discovered would have been too great. Besides, when the information they were gathering was made public, Canada's squeaky, clean image would be no more. It was about time!

And when one of them fell, the others would fall as well. Bet on it! From there, it was just a matter of time until the hydroelectric companies would join the rush to get out of town.

He could hardly believe his good fortune at the documentation these guys were digging up! Why the hell would they have even kept this stuff? In a word, Arrogance! They weren't even worried about being caught! Or taken to task!

Over the next couple of months the pile grew. Files on every despicable act that they had perpetrated. Risk Assessments that were clearly tampered with. Files upon files of payoffs. Some to the locals, most to officials of every stripe. The more they dug, the more they found. It wouldn't be long until they hit the mother lode. When they did, heads would roll! Marcos rubbed his hands together in absolute glee. So very, very close!

33.

I KNOW HE WILL COME BACK TO ME

Karena was convinced that he was still out there somewhere. And that if he could, he would contact her. She just knew it! She knew Marcos was involved somehow. But, and she felt this strongly, her job was to take care of their home and the kids and wait . . . It was hard and her family would constantly beg her to let it go. Move on. But she knew better. And she would wait. She knew that he would have waited for her. That's just the way it was.

Still, not one word. She tried not to let her imagination take over. He would be proud of all that she had accomplished this past while. Their house had truly become a home . . . almost. Until he was there with them it would not be complete. But one day he would be. That is what she would hang onto.

The kids were doing well in school and they were doing great learning English. She was determined to give them the best education that she could. He was big on education and the opportunities it afforded. Wouldn't he be surprised when the kids could speak to him in English! He had done so well learning to speak Spanish. God, I wish he would come home!

He thought of her often, and the kids, and his kids, and he wanted to abandon caution and call her. Just to hear her voice! But he couldn't! If there was one thing he knew, it was that Marcos would follow through with his threats. But one day, he would pay. That was a guarantee!

But it was discouraging. How long would this go on? Surely there had to be a way to contact her! But he knew her. If she ever found out that he was alive, she would spare nothing to find him. He dared not put her in any more danger than she already was.

It's strange how one learns to adapt to their circumstances. That was exactly what they were all doing. They were all survivors and they all knew that life must go on. They would have their time in the sun again one day. To do that, they need believe. And they did. God had brought them together, of that they had no doubt. Each knew the other felt the same. If they had to be separated for a time, well, that's just the way it was. As she always liked to say: " We may be apart for a few months, but we will be together for years." She was always so strong and definitely had both feet planted on the ground. He was strong also, but in a different sort of way. His cup was never less than half full despite the circumstances. He was a dreamer. Sometimes she was sure he lived in some kind of fantasyland! Right now, she wished she was with him! If only he is ok! Please God!

She had to let it go for a while. And not dwell on it. Or it would eat her up. She had the kids to think about. And her Mom. And him. "I know he's alive!"

He would walk through that door one day. Just like he had walked out. Somewhere amidst the tears, she managed a smile.

34.

PANAMA EXPOSED

Those who were passionate about promoting Panama as a first world country could not understand the Indigenous position. How could they not want development? After all, they were the poor of the poor! Surely, anything that would better their economic situation would be a good thing. Wouldn't it? And yet, there they were, protesting, blocking roads, pissing people off! Even getting killed! For what? To protect the environment they say! Their way of life! Please! And hold the rest of us back. If they want a fight, they'll get it. If someone gets hurt or killed, that's their problem!

And this is how it would go. Panamanian against Panamanian. Add in the government and the Indigenous wouldn't stand a chance! Besides, they didn't know what was best for them anyway. It was obvious! The foreigners were pumping billions of dollars into their economy already, and there was more to come. We need to take care of the "Indigenous problem" now before it becomes even worse!

That's how it went down there. And yet, the powers that be severely underestimated their "enemy" and that would ultimately prove to be a fatal mistake. Their "enemy?" These were their people, their heritage, and now they were their" enemy?" But not all of the Panamanians saw it that way. In fact, very few saw it that way at all.

Billions pumped into their economy and yet the average guy on the street was living in poverty or close to it. The rich and powerful became even richer and more powerful. They looked down upon their own people as they might a dog. The people were afraid. So, they nodded their head in agreement during day light hours, but when day turned to night, they joined the protests. Their government and corruption were synonymous. It mattered not what they said or did, they were not to be trusted. This was not the 1st or 100 time that agreements had been made and then busted. Money and favours passing hands is far more powerful than the mere will of the people. Screw them! They need to know their position! They serve us, not us that serve them! Democracy? Right!

Foreigners were pumping billions into the Panamanian economy. They expected to be well rewarded. After all, that's what they were promised. Rules and regulations? Red tape? Not to worry! It was all under control. That's what they were told and nothing less would suffice. It certainly wasn't their problem how they handled their own internal problems. Responsibility? Of course they had some. Why do you think all these do gooders were here helping the poor? Gotta look good on the world stage. Beyond that? Hey, let free enterprise do its thing. We know what we're doing!

When the left hand doesn't know what the right hand is up to it can make for some very interesting times. That's what was happening here. The perfect storm was developing right under their noses.

The government of the day was making and breaking agreements at will. Sweetheart arrangements with foreign interests ensured plenty of "fat" for all who were feeding at the trough. NGO's and charity groups and mission groups whose sole purpose was to help those most in need were being used by the very hands that were feeding them. Marcos was determined to save "his" country at all costs, despite the cost to his own people. People like Cam had now become believers despite the fact that they had been forced against their will. And let's not forget the mining companies themselves, let alone the hydroelectric companies, and other foreign interests whose sole purpose was not to "help," but to make a buck, in fact, many bucks. Besides, it wasn't their problem. Let the government deal with that!

Information was being gathered. Positions were being staked out. Some were moderate. Some were not. Few knew the exact position of the other. And it would have been unlikely that they could have gotten together in any event.

So, they all had their own agendas, and the Indigenous were on the front lines, like it or not. Not all would sympathize with them. Especially not the government and the foreign companies who had their own agenda, aided and abetted by the powers that be. And the business community loathed them as well.

But, the world would be watching this unfold and they would have their say. Woe to the mining companies and others who would rape them. And woe to the government that's best before date had expired.

Panama stable? No! Regardless of what you read.

35.

LET THE GAMES BEGIN

It was time. The documents were leaked. At first to the Ngobe-Bugle. Strategically. Marcos' plan was being set in motion. Get the natives riled up, and when necessary, poke them from time to time to get them really angry. And that's what happened.

They finally had hard evidence. Evidence that even the government couldn't ignore. This time they would be well organized. And they would make sure that the world was watching.

Marcos' people were strategically placed. Some among the indigenous, and some who had infiltrated various levels of government. And he still had his Canadian operative working his magic with some rogue employees of the Kan Mining Corp.

The indigenous were learning to play the game, and play it well. One thing they knew was that they wanted average Panamanians on their side. So, they announced a specific date when they would set up their blockades. They released press releases explaining their position. They urged the locals to stock pile as much as they could. They apologized well in advance for the inconvenience that they knew was to come. They pleaded for their understanding. Never had they been so well organized so far in advance.

But the government was determined to stop them in their tracks before they could gain any momentum. They too, had moles among the indigenous, and they would ferret out the leaders and separate them from the pack. They had too much to lose and they would not let them get the upper hand.

They were aware that the eyes of the world were watching them and they would have to handle this delicately. If it meant breaking a few heads or helping a few people relocate, it would be done. And they had the people to do it.

Marcos could barely contain himself. He had dreamed of this time for so very, very long, and now it was coming to pass. He knew the government had spies placed among the natives. What the government didn't know was that someone else was pulling the strings. That's exactly how he wanted to play it. If they thought the Indigenous were their problem, well, that was perfect. When the time was right, he would rise and drive this government from the land.

So documents would mysteriously find their way into the hands of the indigenous, and some would be leaked to various media outlets. As the government would contain one situation, others would suddenly appear. It was becoming a nightmare. And this was weeks before the announced protests were to take place. It was imperative that they get to some of these leaders and take them out without drawing more attention to themselves.

But Marcos would have none of that. His insiders were doing a great job and as soon as a plan was put in place, he would know about it. They would come up empty handed every time. He loved it! He knew the time was coming when sacrifices would have to be made. A few of his people would likely die. In fact, he knew they would, seeing as how he would be pulling the strings. Oh well! All for the greater good! His, at least!

So the government could do nothing but bandage the situation. They could not afford to upset the foreigners too much. They needed them as much as the foreigners needed them. They put their collective heads together to try and dissuade the Indigenous from staging country wide protests. Offer them whatever you have to until we can get to their leaders. Send in more NGOs and Doctors, nurses, or whatever. Anything! But do it now!

So the Indigenous came from all over Panama. They came from the highlands and they came from the lowlands. They left their homes and headed to the highways and byways across the land. There would be no denying them this time. The world media were notified and present. This would become a defining time in Panama's history. Tens of thousands of protestors would join together. They would be organized, and they would be non-violent but they would stand their ground.

The police would await their masters' orders. Confusion reigned supreme. Orders would be issued, and suddenly rescinded. Over and over again. There were too many eyes on every move that was being made. They didn't want to come off as uncaring or unsympathetic to their own people. And they fought among themselves. It became obvious that winners would be few and that damage control would be the best they could hope for. Kid gloves were required and this was a government used to getting its way whatever they had to do. So hundreds of police were assigned to the various blockades and instructed to do nothing but watch and record, and not resort to violence under any circumstance.

Unheard of in this country. Restraint by the government. Marcos was not impressed. He needed the police to resort to their usual tactics and incite the natives. The eyes of the world were watching and they would be given a story, and that was a guarantee he could provide.

So roads were blocked across the nation and the Indigenous and their supporters would not budge. The police would surveil the protestors from a distance. Many of them were sympathizers but afraid to cross over. Repercussions would be swift and their families would suffer. That's the way it had always been and would always be. That's just the way it is down here.

Fine! Marcos would not be denied. So, let the games begin! The mercenaries were called in and assigned to the most important blockades . He had spent months ensuring he had the best of the best. They would blend in well with the police forces. Each one was a professional and knew his mission. In and out. They knew who their marks were and they knew it had to be done so that the police would be blamed for everything.

The targets were hand picked and 12 protestors would not go back to their families after this day ended. Each sniper would be dressed as a policeman. Then disappear. And all hell would break loose!

Luis was the first to fall. The bullet ripped through his chest and as he fell the crowd scattered. And as they fled, 3 more of them were felled. As the ground turned crimson, the cameras recorded it all for the world to see. History would be made this day in Panama.

Near Bocas the same scene was being played out. Three more were cut down in their prime. Each one had been marked, each one a leader in the movement, and now each one, dead.

These assaults were well planned and well executed. Colon would join its neighbours and 2 more would not go home again. Chaos would reign supreme.

There would be 3 more killed on this day at the last selected site. 12 in all would fall this day. All at the hand of Marcos. For the good of the country. And for the good of Marcos. The government and the police would be blamed for it all. If he had orchestrated this correctly the world would unanimously condemn this government and the multinationals would trip over each other fleeing the country.

Panama would implode and heads would roll. Then he would emerge as the saviour. He had spent his lifetime preparing for this and he would not be denied. "I AM THE ONE!"

These were professional hit men and they had done their homework. Thanks to the advance notice given by the Indigenous as to the location of the blockades, their job was made easy. Vantage points were perfected. All they had to do was wait. Subjects were identified and the long wait would begin. When they got the word they would know what to do. And they did. They were well paid for their effort. Just another day; just another job. Nothing personal.

Except that it was personal to the families of the lost, and to the Panamanian people at large, and to the world. The world would unite with the Panamanians. The Indigenous would not be called as such; they were Panamanians and as a nation they would be united. Ordinary people would have their say.

Where there had been peace, there would be no more. Now, guns, and spears, and machetes would be taken up by all who dared to bear arms.

Foreigners would flee the country, and they would leave with nothing but the shirts on their backs. Where there had been a forced stability, in its place was instability, chaos, and anarchy.

Most of the hatred was directed at their own government but a gringo would be wise to keep a very low profile. Lawlessness was rampant, and indeed, the police force was decimated by desertion. It was a time to distance oneself from the gangs that roamed the streets.

Lest we forget, the mining and hydro-electric companies would not escape the wrath of the people either. Indeed, they were fleeing the country. For good reason. Because on that day of slaughter of the protestors, certain executives of selected companies were also meeting their maker. Once again, the snipers had done their homework. They came and carried out their assigned tasks and disappeared as if they were never there.

Aaron knew about the blockades. And he knew that Marcos was planning something big. Really big, if the rumours could be believed. He knew that he was involved a hell of a lot more than he wanted to be. But nothing could have prepared him for what was now taking place.

Reports were coming in of random killings, unprovoked attacks by the police. Which made no sense. Unless you knew Marcos. And he had opened Pandoras Box.

Sacrifice a few for the greater good. Marcos had preached that message over and over. Aaron knew that the police had not indiscriminately shot dozens of protestors. And he knew that Marcos had. A chill went down his spine. Oh my God! This is really happening! He became afraid. Very afraid. Not just for himself or her, but for Panama.

He was right to be afraid. They laid out their dead. The eyes of the world were watching. This was not an assault on the Indigenous but an assault on Panama. By their own government. There had been endless confrontations and the odd death from time to time but never like this. It made no sense. The government went into full denial. But they were not believed.

But, in this case, they were telling the truth. But their treatment of the Indigenous was well known, and they would suffer the fate of the guilty. And Marcos smiled.

But this day was not yet finished and there would be more bloodshed. Protestors took their anger out on the police forces with a vengeance that would make no one proud. Young police men, merely doing their jobs this day, would be violently attacked and some would be killed.

They were innocent but would become sacrificial lambs. One day they, along with the others would be referred to as martyrs, but today was not that day.

Not only Panamanians would fall this day. In fact, Panama City would become host to a slaughter on this day. A slaughter of 6 top mining executives whom had gathered for a conference with their Panamanian counterparts at the swanky Newport Hotel. This had been long in the planning and promised to be a watershed event which would usher in a whole new approach to the longstanding feud that now existed with the Indigenous.

Was it coincidence that this meeting was scheduled for this exact day? Maybe. Maybe not. But perfect, none the less. They lined them up against the wall, every one of them. When they were done, not one could give testimony to what had taken place. Panama trembled, and the world wept with them.

For carnage ruled the day. The government knew not the enemy. The people blamed the government but nothing made any sense. Many innocents would die this day, victims of a country gone mad.

When they took up their positions at the blockades, the Indigenous knew that violence was a real possibility. Even though they had been instructed not to do so, some among them defied their leaders and carried whatever weapons they could hide on their person. Many of those weapons would find their mark on the flesh of another before this day ended.

They had hoped that this would be a day of reconciliation and new beginnings but few believed it possible. They were right. They sat on a powder keg and it was set to explode. And there was nothing they could do about it.

Luis had beaten the odds. One of the few who had graduated from the University of Panama. Then he returned to his tribe, the Ngobe-Bugle, where he felt he could be a harbinger of change. He quickly rose through the ranks and became a respected leader in the movement. The government was wary of this man and with good cause. He was well educated and had become a media darling. As a result, dangerous. Now, dead. Jose and Andres would die that day as well. They had decided to hang out with their buddy for the day. And their mothers cried.

The meeting in Panama City was a big deal. Finally, there was a chance that they could all get on the same page. Protests or not, this meeting would take place . . . but it didn't.

There was nothing unusual when the waiters entered the room with their cart. That is, until they locked the door behind them and removed their weapons. When they lined them up along the wall they knew what was about to happen. And they were right.

Once again Marcos had struck. But no one knew who the perpetrators were. When they tried to enter the meeting room they found it locked. When security finally made their way into the room, they were met by a sea of blood and 12 bodies, all with a single gunshot to the back of the head.

32 lives were lost on this day. Hundreds more were wounded. Among the dead were 4 members of the Kunas, 8 of the Ngobe-Bugle tribe, another 6 Panamanians, and 6 Canadians as well as 8 police officers.

Chaos ensued. And fingers were pointed. Nothing made sense. The government turned on itself and the snake began to eat its tail. Heads began to roll. The indigenous and the population at large would rise up en masse but they knew not for sure who their enemy was. And Canada stood on guard. Diplomats were sent scurrying. Answers were not forthcoming and the country was set to implode. The world at large braced for the inevitable onslaught. Fear enveloped this land and no one would be safe.

Foreigners fled as best they could. Those unfortunate enough to be caught in hell's fury would not be spared. No one would be declared innocent on this day!

Marcos, from his throne on high, took it all in. Let chaos reign a bit longer. Then the country would be ready for what he had to offer. And he had lots of help. He hadn't just existed in the US. He had begun a process over 20 years ago that would come to fruition in the coming days. He had made a lot of "friends" over the years. Friends in high places, particularly in the US and friends within the political arena post Noriega. They were ready to take back what was rightfully theirs.

Noriega and his ilk were ultimately deposed and Panama began the long climb towards democracy. Successive governments came and went, and though change would take place, Marcos and company felt they should have been the rightful heirs. Corruption still ruled the day and foreigners set the rules. Government after government acquiesced. It became obvious that Panama needed his type of leadership. Since Panama didn't seem to get it, they would put their plan into motion. If it worked as expected, they would have everyone fighting everyone else. The best way to get this going was to stir up the Indigenous. The mining companies were polluting their waterways and the peoples' way of life was being threatened. Health issues were in abundance. The government was complicit. After all, they were letting the foreigners have privileges that their own people were denied. Add in the governments use of their police and para-military units, usually against their own people. Stir a little or a lot if necessary. When all hell broke loose, Marcos could emerge as the great hope of the nation. A peace maker loved by all. Seemed perfectly logical to him!

Canada was in shock. 6 of theirs slaughtered. And no was talking. No one! For God's sake, these were mining people! What did they have to do with anything? Actually, everything! Now they had paid the ultimate price! The money changers saw their investment going down the drain. So sorry about the lost lives. But, more importantly, how would they explain the multimillion dollar losses to their shareholders! Canada was not alone. The world was watching. It soon became apparent that not all was as it seemed. It rarely is.

Cam Henderson was among the lost. He wasn't even supposed to be at that meeting, but at the last minute, they asked him to come along. He was an integral part of their operations down here, and it was time to get him more involved.

After all he had been through these past years, and given his present predicament, it seemed only fitting that he would be in that room. And that he would pay the ultimate price. But at least he would die with a clear conscience. The same couldn't be said about everyone in that room.

But dead they were. All of them. They all had people who cared about them and now they were gone. When word reached our man about Cam and the others, he could contain himself no longer. He slipped out unnoticed into the night. This would prove to be another pivot point in his life.

36.

GO NOW!

Karena had stocked up with as many supplies as she could afford a few days earlier. At least she knew when the protests would begin this time and that shortages were a certainty, and she wasn't about to let that happen to them.

She was afraid. The tension in the air could be cut with a knife and it was unsafe even for regular folk. She dares not send the kids to school despite the governments' assurances.

Then the phone rang. And it was him. "Take the kids and go. You know where. Tell no one! Do you have the other phone?" "Yes!" I will be in contact." Then he was gone. She stared at this phone gone dead. Then she sprang into action. Everything she could take she stuffed into the car and they were gone.

She knew what he meant. That cabin they had rented so very long ago near Puerto Armuelles. Right on the ocean. They had fallen in love with this little hideaway back then, and whenever they could , they would return to it again and again. It was only 3 hours away and those roads would be accessible for sure. If need be, they could slip across the border into Costa Rica if safety became an issue.

"Oh my God! I can't believe it! He's alive!" She cried and she laughed hysterically until she had to pull over. Then she lost it. And the kids were afraid. But she composed herself and she held them close, and she told the kids about him and they cried, and they laughed and they hugged and they danced right there on the side of the road. They asked a hundred questions about him. But she had no answers.

All she knew for sure was: He's alive and he's coming home! "Oh my God!"

It was late when they finally arrived. And they were beat. So off to bed for the kids and then she unloaded their life from the car. Here they would stay until they heard from him. She could not wrap her head around it. Nothing for months on end, and then in a matter of seconds he had reappeared and then disappeared again. Try as she might, and as tired as she was, sleep would not come to her this night. Where was he? Why hadn't he contacted her earlier? Yet she knew not to do this to herself. She knew better, and she knew that one day she would have her answers. But right now, she just wanted to wrap her arms around him and never let him go! But, the pillow would have to suffice yet again, as it had so faithfully done these many months.

His Canadian family hadn't heard from him in such a long time. What they saw on the news terrified them. Panama had reverted to a police state; mass killings were taking place, Canadians were among the victims. And they couldn't get hold of Karena. They were afraid for her and the kids. They knew their Dad was out there somewhere. Was he alive? Surely he would have contacted somebody if he were able to. Now this!

Guaranteed, when they saw him again they would give him a piece of their mind! If he thought that they would visit him in Panama, well, forget that! Please just come home Dad. Please let us know that you're alright. Please!

He did. He contacted them. Briefly. And swore them to secrecy. One slip of the tongue and He or Karena and the kids would be dead. When he could, he would contact them again. Sorry, forgive me, but that's all I can tell you. And they hugged each other and they wept. Then they went about their business.

Had he done the right thing? Wouldn't he want to know if the situation was reversed? Of course he would! he should have done it earlier, but he was afraid for them. Especially for Karena and the kids! That psychopath had threatened to kill them if he didn't co-operate and he knew where they lived!

He was pretty sure that they would be safe at the cabin as long as they stuck to themselves. As long as he went along with Marcos, they wouldn't even think to check on his family. It was going to be difficult here on in. Somehow he had to convince his captors that he was still a soldier in their army. He knew his soul hung in the balance.

He'd gotten to know Cam pretty well and despite their rather peculiar relationship, he was really going to miss that guy. Cam had come full circle. In fact, he was one of the good guys, and now he was dead. At the hands of Marcos!

He had met those other victims as well. At a gala in Panama City when he'd first been "planted" so he could get to know the "who's who of the mining world." They hadn't become friends like Cam. But they were every bit as dead! What the hell was he doing down here? And mixed up with Satan himself, no less.

But of course that wasn't the end of the story. If there even was an end. He knew that at any moment Marcos might decide that he was expendable. After all, he had more than enough documentation to prove to the world just exactly what the mining companies were up to down here. So, why did he need him anymore?

And Marcos thought of "his Canadian." What a job he had done for him! He had practically single handed delivered the death knell for foreign mining in Panama! Of course, he had masterminded that little massacre in Panama City! So the Canuck couldn't take all the credit! Still, there was something different about him this past while. He claimed to be a foot soldier in Marcos' army but he was acting a bit odd. Sure would hate to lose him, but sacrifices have to be made for the greater good. Have to think about that one for a bit.

He didn't really want to have him killed, even though that made the most sense. He liked this guy. They had spent a lot of time together at the beginning. They had cruised along the canal at night and they had eaten at some fine restaurants. he had shown him some of the finer discos in PC, although he didn't seem to be all that interested. That woman in David proved to be a bit of a distraction. If that didn't sort itself out pretty soon, he'd have to arrange something. But, fortunately, it worked out even better than he planned. "I bet we could have been great friends in another life!" And he chuckled.

But, he had bigger fish to fry on this day. The government was ready to collapse; the indigenous were returning to their homes and confiscating whatever they could from the abandoned mines; the US was threatening everybody as usual, and the shop keepers were arming themselves to keep their neighbours at bay.

So, it was time. In the days ahead, he would make his move. They couldn't really call it a coup. Yet, a coup by any other name is still a coup!

Aaron knew that he had been used, and that Marcos would no longer be requiring his "services." He knew he wasn't responsible for what had taken place in Panama City but he definitely was involved in getting the "goods" on the mining companies. And though they deserved to fall, this was abominable! He was pretty sure that Marcos would be cleaning up any loose ends, and he was definitely a loose end!

He needed to talk to Karena. He needed to explain these past months as best he could. And somehow explain why he didn't contact her sooner. She had no idea how dangerous Marcos could be. He did, and he hoped she would understand. Nonetheless, he would figure out something, and if he could, he would go to her. How to do that without attracting attention, he did not know.

Obviously Marcos was unsure about this gringo as well, and his "soldiers" were keeping a pretty close eye on him these days. Crap! And she was a good eight hours away from his prison.

But a plan began to formulate. She had kept his old phone activated. She'd always left minutes in it and left it with the kids so they could reach her if something ever happened. They had often joked that they would always have a way to keep in touch even if the whole world tried to keep them apart. God, I wonder if she had expected to hear from him that way if something went wrong. He had completely forgotten that, in fact, he had forgotten almost everything. But now it would be their life line.

He dialled the number . . . and he held his breath . . . ring . . . ring . . . ring . . . nothing, and then he heard it. A small, quiet voice "hello," and he knew it was her! "It's me. I can't talk long. Can you talk?"

"Can I talk? Oh my God! Yes! Where are you? Are you coming home?" His heart sank. He missed her so but he knew what he had to say would not go over well. So he let her talk, and talk, and talk some more. Question after question after question, and he had no satisfactory answers. But still . . . he loved listening to her, even when she was angry. This was one passionate Panamanian, no doubt about it! But she was scared, and pleaded with him to come home. "I miss you, the kids miss you. Please come home!"

He knew it was impossible. There was no escaping the long arm of Marcos. If he ever found them he would slaughter them. He had made that abundantly clear!

He tried to explain that to her but she would have none of it. "We've been through so much together. Come home and we'll figure it out together. "She just didn't get it! "This is different. He will kill you if he gets the chance! Don't you understand that?"

Of course she did. But she was a fighter, this one. "Come home and we'll slip across the border into Costa Rica. He'll never find us. Please! We need to be together. Maybe we could make it to Canada. I don't care. Just as long as we are together!" He knew she was crying, and whether she knew he was or not, he could not tell, and all he could think about was pulling her in through that phone and wrapping his arms around her and never letting go!

So they hatched a plan that night, and in one weeks' time they would make their break. He would escape his captors and make his way to her, and from there, they would slip over the border. And hang low for as long as necessary. And pray that no one turned them in. It was a big gamble but at least they would be together. So, she would ensure that she had plenty of minutes in this phone. She would never try to contact him. Instead, be ready, and when he called they would make their bid for freedom.

So they said their "so long, see you later" stuff, but never "good bye." That hadn't worked out to well in the past so they weren't going there again.

He shouldn't have contacted her. God! What was he thinking? And now they were in extreme danger. And it was his fault. Fear gripped this man and his "gut feeling" was usually dead on. A sense of urgency pervaded his very being and he knew he had to act now.

He was unsure how to proceed. They were watching him constantly. Like they knew what he was up to. There was no way he could wait another week. Hell, he may not have another day the way this thing was going, unless, hmmm, unless he was able to create a distraction of some sort, without drawing attention to himself.

So, he figured that the best defence would be an active offence. He had them call Marcos for him. And let him know that he was ready for more assignments. Hopefully he would buy that, at least for a while.

It seemed he had. They told him Marcos wanted to see him in person, and would call him in a couple of days to make arrangements. Yes! That's all the time he would need. Good bye Marcos!

37.

I WIN . . . YOU LOSE!

As if! Marcos had not gotten to where he was by being stupid. If this gringo thought he could pull one over him, then maybe he wasn't as smart as he appeared to be. It was time to deal with this Canuck. He had been such a good soldier.

Then Marcos made a mistake that would cost him dearly. Maybe not today. Maybe not even tomorrow. One day though . . .

Aaron made another call to let her know that they would be moving up the timetable. And to let her know that they may be on to him. If he didn't show up or he wasn't in contact, then she was to do nothing. But wait. He would never let them know that they had been in contact. She should be safe to return home. But never, ever speak of him to anyone. Like she would listen!

So he made his plans. And Marcos made his plans. Only one of these plans would be successful on this day. It would not be his. The puppet master had once again won the day. And lost. Just not yet!

They took him by force, and they beat him to within an inch of his life, and they threw him into a filthy cell, and they left him to rot. But they didn't kill him. Marcos, in his twisted, sick world had decided to spare him. After all, he liked this gringo! Let's see how well he was doing in a few months! Then he'll decide his fate. After all, he was god, wasn't he?

38.

BEATEN . . . NOT BROKEN

Daily, he had been beaten mercilessly. Within an inch of his life he had come and still they didn't quit. He would not escape the darkness, not yet. But though they broke his body and tormented his soul, they could not break his spirit.

He had refused to cooperate with his captors, and try as they might, he would not bend. How they knew not of his southern family he did not know, but incredibly, they didn't or they just didn't care. Obviously, Marcos thought that the Panamanian lady he was seeing was just a fling,(thank God he had never mentioned her name) or he could have been broken early on. So if die he must, then die he would. But he would die honourably. Nobody else would know, but, he would.

But why had they kept him so long? Why were they releasing him now? Nothing made sense. Or, did it? He was dead in most people's eyes already. Why not finish the job?

Drugs had never been his thing. Hell, he rarely even drank, until he met Marcos, that is, but now, he was heavily addicted to heroin. Marcos ensured his dependence on them, and they had succeeded. To a point. "I let you live, didn't I?" So, they won, at least for now.

He was stuck in this hell with no end. But something had happened. A changing of the guard, perhaps. He had waited for Sammy to deliver him into the netherworld once again but he did not come. No one came, and he languished in agony days on end. No reprieve, no nothing! Surely he was dying. They had left him to rot in his own filth. Then it happened. And he felt strangely alive. Alone but alive. The convulsions had stopped, and although weak and dehydrated and hungry, he began to remember. He began to remember a lot.

So when they came for him and demanded he write a letter to his family demanding 50,000 US dollars be wired to an offshore account, he knew he had to leave something in the letter lest they drugged him again, something to tie it all together. Where they would ever get that much money he hadn't a clue! And besides, what guarantee was there that they'd let him go anyway? In any case, here are some excerpts from that letter: (I don't know where to begin. I am so sorry that I couldn't contact you earlier but I couldn't . Please believe me, this is no joke. I need you to send 50,000 US dollars to the following account xxxxxxxxxxxxx and then they will put me on a plane to Canada. Do not contact the authorities. If the money is not in the account by xxxxxxxxxx, you will not be seeing me again. I need to come home. I am very ill and cannot last much longer without help. They are treating me well but there is no medicine. Please) . . .

They wanted him gone. Sooner rather than later. They checked the letter but they questioned him not. Get him the hell out of here. Why the hell Marcos didn't just have him killed made no sense at all! It wasn't like he needed the money . Confused, beaten, but not entirely broken, Aaron would soon find himself back home with his family. His Canadian family.

He thought about Sammy. And he thought about Jerry. This was the only companionship he had for over a year. Then they just dumped him on the plane like a sack of potatoes. Like a piece of garbage! He was nothing but a job to them. It was pretty obvious that if they had been asked to kill him, that it wouldn't have bothered them for a second! But, he was alive. And that's all that counted right now.

Sammy had taken care of him, between beatings, that is. Yeah, he beat him but then he would give him his fix, and, it worked. He talked to him, almost like an equal. But, he never saw Sammy, as he always wore a hood. At least he seemed to care.

Jerry was another story. He was instantly afraid, again. He remembered now why he called him Jerry. Nazi he was, and Aaron was his experiment gone wrong. He had beaten this man unto death nearly, yet he would not break. As the punishment became more and more severe, and the drugs less and less effective, Aaron thought he would surely die. And yet, when almost all hope was gone, Sammy would step in and coax him into a fantasyland fuelled by heroin. So it would go, night after night, month after month, and finally into the second year. Why him? Why?

But, they had their orders, to the brink of death, no more. If he died, they died. Simple as that. And then it was over. The money arrived and they sent him home. Didn't even say goodbye! But what Aaron didn't know was that the order to send him back to Canada hadn't come from Marcos at all. Hell, Marcos had abandoned them also! They were just going to shoot him and get the hell out of there, that is, until they came up with their own plan. Any loyalty that they had to Marcos was long gone. Jerry had set up an offshore years ago when he was "involved" in certain, shall we say, illegal activities. He had funnelled funds there on occasion, and knew it was "safe" from prying eyes. Marcos might have treated him like a fool but he would have the last laugh! And now they would wait. If the money actually arrived, he would dispose of this gringo once and for all. And as for Sammy, well, he had a bullet with his name on it as well. Sorry, friend!

And then it arrived! Incredible! Time to dispose of these two and get the hell out of here! But, not yet. Sammy had other plans.

"We need to get him on a plane. Otherwise, we're just as bad as Marcos!" If he only knew!

So Jerry played along. Get him out of here and then deal with Sammy. He had to chuckle. "What an idiot!" Aaron would never know it, but Sammy had just saved his life!

39.

SENT BACK TO CANADA

They recoiled at the sight of him. He had always been so healthy and now he was emaciated. His cheeks were hollow, he was grey, and obviously full of disease. They barely knew him anymore. He was always "different" but now he had become distant as well. Oh, he was polite, respectful, and definitely interested in the lives of those around him, but something was off. Whatever had happened during those missing years had changed this man, and if they thought they hadn't known him previously, well, now it was impossible. And though close, he was very far away. They knew that he missed her, though he spoke not of her, and when the letter arrived from her, they knew he would soon go. In some ways, that was a good thing. He had said so very long ago that he didn't belong here, and reluctantly, they had to agree. Now she wanted him to come "home." Her words. They knew he would go. He did. And they mourned their fallen son, brother, dad, friend, for wherever he was, he was not here any longer.

They had had no word for such a long time, and now he was returning to the scene of the "crime." It made no sense! They hung their heads and mourned their loss. And wondered aloud if this would be the last time they saw him alive.

He knew what they were thinking. There was nothing he could say that would appease them. He felt bad, and guilty. He knew they felt abandoned and probably rightly so. But he couldn't stay, and even if she had not reached out to him, he knew his time at home would be short. He knew he had something to do. Some unfinished business. Somewhere deep inside his disturbed mind lay the answers. Someone needed to pay. And they would. Just not yet. And there was a little matter of 50,000 dollars that he fully expected to return to its' rightful owners!

PART TWO

40.

AARON RETURNS TO PANAMA . . . AGAIN

Karena worked with him as best she could. They began to work through the quagmire of his mind. It was difficult. He was frustrated but determined to know the truth. As the truth emerged, she knew not if she could stay by his side. For this was surely not the man she had fallen in love with. Still . . .

This would continue for many months. This man strong and virile one moment; a broken and shattered man the next. But she could not leave him alone. It took everything in this woman and God himself to still the waters. A strong faith had always been his forte, but now, the darkness was pervasive, and his faith severely compromised. Had he only realized that it was that faith that had allowed him to survive this long. In fact, it would ultimately bring him back from the brink of hell. He knew that hell was real. He had surely lived it, and knowing he must return to it to conquer his demons was unimaginable! Yet he must. And he did.

Exhaustion became his companion, and with each passing day his reality become more and more distorted. She knew not how to help him and soon became afraid. Afraid for him but also for the kids and herself. She knew this man well and he would never hurt her or the kids, that she was sure of. Still, she had never seen him like this. But she couldn't go. He had stood by her in the worst of times and she would not abandon him now.

The tension grew, and the nightmares grew ever more menacing, and she could hide her fear no longer. He knew. He asked her to leave him, to just go. He loved this woman so, and yet he knew not himself or what he was capable of. So she left. And he cried, and he called out to God as never before.

As he slowly slipped into the abyss he put pen to paper once more, like he had done throughout the years, and he wrote, and he recorded his every thought. Surely to God, within this framework the answers would lie. Just give me something to hang onto Lord, anything!

There were nuggets hidden in the recesses of his mind, and as he jotted down his thoughts, he began to remember. Yesterday began to come into focus. He remembered his blogs of yesteryear and he dug them out as well. Like pieces in a puzzle trying to find their way home these nuggets of his life befriended him and the puzzle began to take form.

For the first time in a very long time, he laid his head down and he slept. Then he called her. And she knew that he was back. Not completely, but he was on his way home.

So she went to him. Again. He knew she was there. They would find this demon and destroy it. She had lost him once, and almost lost him a second time, but no more. They had been through so much to be together and they would not be denied. This was to be a battle of epic proportions and it would take everything they had in them and the good Lord himself to bring this to its' proper conclusion.

That letter he had written . . . could he have left a clue in it? As he studied the letter and what he had written, he began to sense the text between the lines. He had been home for many months and it had not even crossed his mind, and yet now, it was front and centre.

It all started coming back; a fragment here, a morsel there, and slowly a picture began to emerge. It stopped him in his tracks. Fear overtook this mere mortal, and anxiety once again became his constant companion.

When he penned that letter he was under guard and watched less he say something that could be traced back to them. Yet he had to try and now he searched that very letter. Surely he had left some kind of clue. He had to have! Over and over he reread that letter. Then he remembered something and he cried out in agony, and as the sweat and tears became as one, he collapsed and could not be consoled for days.

Karena thought she had lost him yet again, this behemoth of a man; yet so fragile. But she stayed with him and held him as a mother might hold a child. She loved this man and nothing, absolutely nothing, would steal him away from her again. So she nursed him back from the brink once again. Slowly but surely it would all begin to make sense.

41.

I WILL STAND BY YOU

Circumstance had ripped these two apart and circumstance would once again unite them. As she worked with him to navigate the mine fields of his mind, she could not suppress her anguish at what was being revealed. This was such a strong man, yet the salvage gathered was from the distorted mind of another. She had known him a long time by now, perhaps not by others' standards, but they knew each other well. It was like they had always known the other. She was taken aback, time and time again by what was being revealed.

She would find herself studying this man. Analyzing him as a psychologist might, and she felt guilty. He wasn't just some "subject" to be studied. This was the man that she had fallen in love with. This was the man that stood by her when darkness threatened to envelope her very existence. This was the man who had changed his entire life to be with her. And though she too had made sacrifices to be with him, he had given up his entire life and look where it had gotten him. Gotten them. And she blamed herself. He wouldn't be in this spot had they not got involved. But damn! They had got involved and they knew that if they must, they would go to hell and back for the other. So he was in hell and she was taking that ride with him. They knew that the God they knew would never abandon them. Even though it felt like it now. For something, or someone had led him back home to her.

And that is what they would call on. Their faith. It had sustained them thus far and the devil himself was unable to keep them apart. They would explore the far regions of his mind gone mad and destroy the monster that dwelled within. If anyone knew these two, they would know that they would not quit. And they didn't. There would be unhappy endings for some if they had their way!

42.

AND THE MIND REVEALS

Almost anything could set him off. What had they done to him? He was such a strong man, and yet, it was if he were a child. It was hard. She had come to rely on him so much. He was always so sure of himself. With him she had always felt protected. But now, he was lost. She needed him desperately but right now, he needed her.

Right from the beginning they had this symbiotic relationship. Neither knew why or how it had grown us quickly. But they knew it had. They knew that together they could withstand anything. Had they not stood against well-meaning families who would tear them apart? Had either of them weakened, they would have never known the other as they do now. Yet, one of them was now missing in action, and it was up to the other to mount a rescue mission and bring that person home. And she would.

And though incapable now, this man would one day tell all who would listen, of this heroic woman who God himself had chosen to be by his side. He would mean it. And they would know that it was so.

He would fight his demons. As best he could. She by his side. It would be a long and hard battle. It would have been so much easier to give up. But she would not let him! He resented her for that. And he loved her for that! Alone he could take no more. But together they could do this.

43.

AND STILL HE RULED

And the truth was revealed, and the extent of his involvement left them both astounded. How could this man have succumbed to such a degree that he had become a different person. Was that even possible? Yet, here they were, and he had indeed been front and centre in this movement. Like it or not!

So what now? She just wanted them to go home. They had sacrificed blood, sweat, and tears to stake out their claim and now that was gone. But they were alive, and they were together. Surely, if what they had gone through meant anything, it was that they were survivors. They would rise again. And they would rebuild their home, together. As long as Marcos was still on the scene, their lives were in jeopardy. Panama was in chaos so Costa Rica would call itself home for a time.

They had been forcibly separated on two previous occasions. One, a few months, the other, much, much longer, and she was not about to let this happen again. They would stay together and ride out whatever came their way.

A lot had changed while he was incarcerated. Not all bad. Yes, the country had been thrown into chaos. Marcos had not become the "king" but had become a "king maker." But it turned out he didn't know his "king" quite as well as he thought. That would lay the foundation for the beginning of the end. Marcos had unleashed his demons on Panama. The government had fallen. His man had assumed the leadership of a conglomerate of disenchanted and disenfranchised people. Much good was done. But the truth has a habit of coming out. And truth would not be denied. It would take some time but already there were rumblings that much was amiss.

Marcos was becoming a tad uneasy these days. There were whispers, always just out of range, and furtive glances that seemed indicative of, well, he wasn't sure what. His "friends" were becoming conspicuous by their absence. The shadows seemed somehow to come alive, especially when he was alone. He would laugh this off, but he knew that something was terribly amiss.

Information used against the former government and the mining companies had done their deed rather well, but now the questions demanded answers. Who had really revealed this information? When the arithmetic was done, it just didn't add up. Marcos was confused. Why all the questions? This was the new Panama. Leave the past in the past. Move on and celebrate for they would soon be a first world nation! Isn't this what they wanted? "I did it! Me! If not for me Panama would still be in the dark ages. Now you dare to question me? I should be the President!" And the mirror agreed.

So many people had died; ordinary people that were not involved in the politics of the day. No one knew who the real perpetrators were. Suspicion grew, and fingers were even more pointed than usual. Some of those fingers began finding a bulls eye. Its' name was Marcos.

In a land of paranoia and suspicion, anyone and everyone comes under scrutiny. The scrutinizers were many, and eager to cast blame and deflect it away from themselves.

There was much blame to go around. This country had many secrets. As happens so often in these cases, the victims now became the perpetrators and would exact their pound of flesh. All would be unclean and mothers on all sides would cry for their dead children. There is rarely a "right" in all of this; definitely degrees of, but all would have blood on their hands.

It is easy to point at the government, or the mining companies, or the indigenous, and so on, and declare them to be the problem, but that is simplistic at best. In a culture of corruption the ship is not easily turned, and this ship was not unlike many others in this area.

Stories would be told, and many a book written, and dozens of inquiries would dominate this landscape during this tumultuous time, and slowly but surely, key components would be exposed for what they were, and nooses would begin to tighten. And Marcos could feel his neck tie getting ever tighter.

44.

I WILL HAVE MY REVENGE

Aaron was not happy. He was becoming better informed with each passing day. He knew that Marcos' days were numbered. But that was not good enough. After what Marcos had done to him, and his family, and to thousands of others, and with him being complicit, he wanted revenge. And he would get it.

She worried about him. He said he was fine, and that he knew the situation would be resolved by the appropriate parties, but she knew him...well. Whenever he didn't arrive home on time, her heart would skip a beat and she would watch the door for any sign from him. But, he always returned as if nothing was amiss.

Maybe she was wrong. He was writing feverishly, and he was more than adequately providing for them. Actually, life wasn't half bad. If the news could be believed, they may be able to return home in the next few months. What to, she wasn't sure, but whatever it was, they would manage quite fine, thank you very much!

He did provide, and he took great pains to assure her that he was ok, in fact, he was actually pretty good, and he too, was looking forward to returning to their home, modest though it may be.

He knew revenge was not the answer. He knew it went against everything that he believed in, but he was haunted by the images of the deceased which seemed to pervade his being. He felt guilty, and well he should have.

The government was stable; the foreign investors were slowly starting to return to this troubled, but now apparently stable land. The "terrorists," and that's what they were called, were being ferreted out and exposed to the world at large. Justice appeared to be done. Ordinary Panamanians would walk the streets again, and businesses would open and begin to welcome all who came through their doors. It was an uneasy peace, but the will of the people would dominate, and Panama would begin the long, arduous task of rebuilding, not on what was before, but on a foundation built on trust, respect, and integrity.

The foreigners would attempt to conduct business, not as before, but in a transparent manner previously unknown here. Though trust would remain a huge issue, slowly, ever so slowly, a culture of corruption would change its' course. All would benefit. But Marcos would get credit…for nothing. In fact, evidence was mounting rapidly, and it was not looking good for Marcos. Not at all!

Despite all the events of the past few years, the Indigenous would grow ever stronger, and would find their rightful place at the table, and though compromises would be made, all would emerge feeling vindicated and cohesive and forward looking. A strong country would begin to emerge. No longer would it be a facade, or a glossy store front, or a glorious skyscraper, but it would become safe and prudent to peer into the windows or open the doors and find substance behind what had been previously closed doors.

This would not happen without protest. For the money changers of old would not give up their lofty positions so easily, but they could be persuaded, and soon they would find other breeding grounds better suited to their business practices. That would not be hard. Where there is a need, there is greed, and there is much need.

And there is still a great need here, and desperate people do desperate things, but, it is definitely not business as usual.

Aaron despaired. For he knew his thoughts were not "right." Try as he might, he could not shake the utter helplessness that he felt within. He knew he would leave her yet again. And she would surely reach a point where she could take no more. He despaired of losing her, for he loved her as no one before, and yet, he was compelled to face the monster one more time. There would be tragic consequences if he were to follow through. He knew how unfair this was to his family. They, and he, had been through so much.

He knew in his mind that he would go. He couldn't speak for her. But he knew that she knew. And it broke his heart. If he even had one! But the time had come and he had to go.

She knew it. And she hated him for it. And she loved him for it. He was a man of principle. But she wasn't sure she could take any more. They had lived on the edge for so long already. One slip and he was in the abyss, and she wasn't sure she could follow him any longer. But still she kept quiet. Still she loved him and he knew it. Could her love be enough to hold this man back? She knew he loved her dearly but it was as if he were possessed, and indeed he may have been. But still she stayed silent.

When she got up the next morning and he wasn't there, she wasn't surprised. So she made breakfast as usual, minus his dish, and then went about her day. Just another day. But it wasn't.

He had gotten up early that day. He had watched her sleep. Then he left. He went for a long ride that day, a ride that would take him back to an incredible time in his life. And her life. To the place they had met and where they had fallen in love.

He had not planned on getting involved with anyone on this journey. And yet he had. Several times in fact. It had not ended well for any of those involved with him. As he drove and reflected on these past many months, for the first time in a very long while, he gave himself a break. His intentions, in every case, were honourable, and had things turned out differently, a different story would have been written. But they didn't, and he would make decisions that no normal person should have to make. Now it was time to make another decision. He had wanted to wake her to tell her what he was doing on this day, but she looked so peaceful, so he slipped silently out. Let her sleep a little longer. She certainly deserves it.

45.

AND THEY MADE A DECISION

Then he made a decision that would change their course dramatically. A small decision but with big consequences. A simple phone call to tell her where he was and what he was doing. When she answered and he told her what he was up to, she broke into tears. He could hear her anguish through the phone and he knew what she had been thinking! Why hadn't he wakened her? What the hell was he thinking? He knew what he had to do. And he went home.

They talked. And they cried. They vowed to finish this story together. Not he. Not she. But they. The two of them would finish this story together, whatever the consequences.

At long last, they were able to rest. No one would disappear into the night. Never again.

He would exact his revenge on Marcos. But in a way totally unexpected. At least to him. He would, with the help of Karena, rise above his own desires, and for once in his life, he would do nothing. That's right! Nothing illegal, that is. And be a better man for it. But he would do what he could legally to see that this monster never hurt anyone again.

As surely as the darkness had enveloped him, he now saw light in its place. Revenge was replaced by a deep desire to see justice done. She stood by his side and together they would do their part.

46.

MARCOS TAKES HIS LEAVE

Marcos went into hiding. He was bewildered. He was the architect! If not for him, Panama would still be a wanna be nation. Yet look at where it is going now! Now they want to make him out as a criminal? If not for him . . .

He was right. If not for him countless mothers would still have their children, and wives would have their husbands and children their fathers.

If he hadn't orchestrated the events of the past couple of years, Panama, it could be argued, would still be in a constant state of oppression and corruption would still rule the day. It could be argued, but the methodology he employed left no room for discussion. It was simply wrong and it was reprehensible.

He had spent most of his adult life in service to his country. Sadly, he was right about so much, and had he taken a different approach, he may well have gotten the accolades he felt he so richly deserved. Now it was unlikely that he would even live to see his dream fulfilled. He was a marked man and visions of Saddam played verily in his head. For he too was dispatched to an underground bunker, forced underground by the very same people he had brought to power.

When Ricardo was first approached by Marcos, whom he had admired for years, he was deeply honoured that such a man even knew his name. Now he was being asked to head up a new political party. This was a man who had taken on Noriega in his day. He was a hero to many such as himself who had read of these patriots, and now . . . Marcos had originally planned on being President. After all, if it wasn't for him, none of this would have happened. But there were rumblings and there was opposition that he hadn't expected. Now his compatriots in the US were distancing themselves. OK, so he hadn't shared with them his complete plan. He hadn't told them about the contractors. So? Sacrifice a few. Big deal! Except it was. Marcos was given a choice. Be the king maker. Fine. But the king? No. That's where Ricardo came in. Choose him to represent us and keep your dignity. If this thing goes sideways, it's simple. We don't know you! And with that, Marcos approached Ricardo and saved his own sorry ass.

Ricardo decided that he would run, and he would gather the best minds around him. Marcos would become his main adviser. Together they would ensure the downfall of this government and form a government truly representative of the people, all the people. None would be denied entry. Corruption, wherever it reared its ugly head would be dealt with accordingly. He was a realist. You do not change a culture of corruption overnight, but you must start somewhere. There were big fish to fry, and by God, he was ready to fry a few fish! Had he only known that the fish that needed frying the most stood right next to him!

It took very little to convince the masses that he represented their best hope for the future for their beloved country. He was an elegant man, and a persuasive man, and he easily defeated the government and the existing parties of the day. Many would say this was a bad move and based more on fear and popularity than on substance. True it may have been, but victory would be theirs.

Marcos held his head high these days and he took it all in. If not for him . . .

But Ricardo was no dummy either, and he suspected that there was something amiss. Unknown to his key adviser, he began making inquiries and what he was finding out was making him incredibly uneasy. There had long been rumblings regarding Marcos, but he had dismissed it as merely rumour and innuendo perpetrated by those nursing their shattered egos. But still, he had an obligation to follow this to wherever it may go. What he found drove him to his knees! And now he was complicit, a part of something he had vowed to eradicate.

He would not wait long to act. He didn't have all the facts, but he had enough! And this hero of his would fall. "Mark my words!" So he summoned his "hero" that they may discuss the strategies of the coming weeks and months. But Marcos didn't come. Then he knew. For sure. So he sent the police for him but he was not to be found.

He would call on the full force of the law to uproot this man wherever he may be, and exact justice not unlike what Marcos had done to countless others! He would come clean to the nation. He prayed they would support him now, even more than ever, and uproot evil wherever it may be found. They did. And he did.

Aaron had kept copies of every document that he had obtained concerning the mining companies; he had the ammunition he required to get the authorities attention. Anonymously, of course. Just enough information to make them want more, to dig a little deeper. They did dig, and what they found led them to a vault full of secrets.

Once you are part of the "spy" world you are never really out. Information would find its way back to our man. He would release documents. To different outlets. Some to the government; some to the media outlets, and some would find their way into opposition political party hands. Enough to keep the pressure on but nothing that could be linked to him. He was becoming very good at this game.

"Ah Marcos, what a fine trainer you turned out to be! Remember how proud you were to share all your secrets with me? Well, they are secrets no more! They're coming for you, Marcos!"

Marcos felt his tie getting ever tighter. He was being treated with less and less respect by those around him. He knew he had to get away. They would either find him or one of his own men would eventually betray him for a sack of gold. Dogs! How dare they! But they dared alright. So he made a plan. He was always good at making plans. But if this one failed, without question, he would be hanged. If he was caught by the wrong group...he shuttered to think of what they might do to him.

They thought him sick. So when the Doctor was summoned, no suspicion was aroused. When the Doctor told those around him that he was contagious and to leave him undisturbed for a couple of days, they were more than happy to comply. So they set up a couple of days supplies for him, and he let them know that he would call them if need be. Otherwise, do not disturb.

And they didn't disturb him. But by day 3, and no word from him, they felt they had no choice but to call the good Doctor. He came over immediately and rushed into the room, Marcos' men by his side. What they found...was nothing! No Marcos! Nothing!

Then reality sunk in, and they knew he had screwed them over just like he had done to everyone else. And they were wanted by the law, these patriots, and mercy was not to be their friend. As the rats attempted to leave the sinking ship, there was much chaos, and there was much fighting, and they began to slaughter each other. Those that did escape were rounded up in quick order, and the letter of the law would be suspended for a time. Everything had changed, and yet, nothing had changed it seemed.

It was obvious to all that the Doctor was involved, and he would pay dearly for his transgressions. Try as he would to explain that he did so under duress, that Marcos had threatened to kill his family if he did not co-operate, his words fell on deaf ears. Though his family would survive, he would not. Just another victim that Marcos would claim.

Marcos was not to be found. Anywhere. Though they searched near and far, victory would not be theirs. In a land of spies it seemed impossible that he could have left the country undetected. If that were so, then where was he?

Word soon reached the streets and the common man would join in the search. Nothing would be overlooked. A nation divided came together to find this man. At all costs! But they didn't!

There is nothing money won't buy, and Marcos had money. Money would buy him escape, and it did. Well placed friends in the US would ensure that he was well hidden. And that is exactly what happened.

47.

SPY I AM

When Aaron heard of this, he knew what he must do. And she knew what he must do. This time they were on the same page. What Marcos didn't know was that his gringo had "come across" some rather interesting paperwork on their last visit. Names, numbers, all US at that. He had copied down every last name and address he could find. Just in case. One never knows when one just might need this kind of information!

This he would not share with anyone. They had come full circle and now the hunter would become the hunted. He would fit in well, this gringo. Hadn't Marcos always said that? Well Marcos, soon you might just find out!

So she bid him farewell once again. But this was different. They were in this together. She knew he was no longer just looking for revenge but that justice be served. He would gather the information necessary to ensure that Marcos would face the people of his country. If he found him, no, when he found him, and set the trap securely, others would be notified. They would expropriate this man, and there would be little protest. For to protest would invite scrutiny, and that was not to their liking.

They knew this could be a mission of many months. There were no guarantees that this had even happened or that these names were of any importance, but his gut begged to differ. He would follow the trail wherever it led him.

He a spy. Had anyone suggested such a thing a few years back, he would have thought them crazy! Actually, if anyone was crazy, it was probably him. But, he was actually pretty good at it, even though he was as old school as they come. When, or if he needed help, there would be plenty available. But this was a time for yesterday's man to do his thing. And he would.

There were but six on this list, and what relation they bore to the other, he knew not. But he would. Eventually. If you feel what you have read to date is nothing more than fantasy, then get ready to be challenged as never before, or put this book aside now. Conspiracy theorists, take note, for where he may have debunked you in the past, or grouped you all together as one, he was forced to acknowledge, as fact, tales he would have outright dismissed in the past.

He began to surveil those on the list. Unfortunately, he was no techno-geek, so this was going to be a long, arduous task. The chances of anyone mistaking him for a spy were unlikely at best. Boston seemed like a strange choice, it seemed to him, to harbour a would be dictator like Marcos. Guess he would find out soon enough. But Marcos had mentioned Boston in one of his diatribes, so who knows!

Out of the house at 7; quick stop at Starbucks; and off to the Generations Health Club. 9 a.m. and he's on the move. Next stop: Jefferson and Associates Law Offices.

He would stake out this place, and he would watch for his target until he appeared. In this case, 4:30 pm. Probably just a guy doing his job.

Maybe he was a fool after all. Oh well, I'm here now. Might as well play this out!

And that he did. The hours turned into days and soon he knew this mans' ritual. He altered it little, and if he had anything to hide, well, he was doing a pretty good job. But, he continued to snap photos and document what little he had. He would send the info back to Karena and she would get it into the appropriate hands.

Then he started to notice something. So he decided to follow through on his hunch; after all, what was there to lose. He sent her the photos of his target and some of the other men that frequented the club every morning. He asked her to check out the names they had against the photos he had taken. Suddenly it began to make sense. One, two, and finally three of the names on Marcos list were frequenting this club at the same time each morning. Then he knew. He was on to something. He didn't know just what, but he smelled a rat.

He now knew their habits well enough to find them whenever he wanted so he moved on. Strange that if the other names that were on his list were associated somehow, that they didn't make an appearance. Oh well, back to work!

He continued to dig. And he continued to hit pay dirt. So he surveilled others on his list and he would not be disappointed. Again there were three who met at the same place each morning, and then went on their separate ways. Much like the others. Again he forwarded on everything of value to Karena, and she in turn, onto the appropriate authorities.

What they had, if anything, remained to be seen. But he felt overwhelmingly convinced that the answers they sought were here. If they could just tie Marcos to one or both of these groups! Besides, he had no proof of any wrong doing anyway. But he was convinced . . .

So he stayed with it. She wanted him to come home but he felt that he was close to a break in the case. He wanted to be here if anything was to go down. It was a good thing he held firm. Because, three days hence, a meeting would take place, and all six of these men would be there. Except there weren't six. There were seven.

And he knew the seventh man intimately. Marcos had finally made an appearance, and any doubt he had, vanished.

So now he had the photos and documentation of times and places. Other than the fact that Marcos was a wanted fugitive in Panama, they really had no proof of anything. No matter. They had time. Someone would make a mistake. They always do. And he had become a very patient man.

He had done his job, rather well, thank you very much, but it was time to pass this info on and let the "real spies" do their thing. And he was glad of it. When he had first spotted Marcos, he had wanted to wrap his fingers around his neck and squeeze the very life out of him. Unfortunately that would have accomplished little. Better that he be brought to justice and made an example of. He would wait, perhaps impatiently, but he would wait for justice to be done.

They would continue to gather information, this invisible network, and what they would discover would shake up the foundations not only of Panama but of every country in Central America! And probably beyond!

Conspiracy theorists would have a hay day. Ironically, they would be right!

48.

HONEY, I'M HOME!

He returned home to Panama where she awaited. She was proud of her man. He had fought his demons and he had won. They had won. Justice would be served. It wouldn't bring back the victims of Marcos' atrocities but it would provide some relief and it would certainly instil confidence that Panama was indeed moving forward. And that was a good thing.

So they settled in once more. The kids were back in school, and she was finally able to settle into the University, which she had so long wanted to return to. One day she would be a professor and help shape the minds of future leaders, and definitely ensure that they learn how to think for themselves. That was a given!

Aaron continued to write, more feverishly than even before. His work was being critically acclaimed. He had become a voice to be heard, a fervent supporter of the new Panama. He may have been a gringo once, but he was now one of them. She found it amusing: he had often said "Just give me a chance and they will soon know who I really am." He was right.

He knew that one day Marcos would be back in Panama; Aaron's comrades on the outside would ensure that. Borders are crossed every day illegally, and he knew that one more crossing would help heal a nation. Welcome Marcos! We're waiting for you!

The world would be mortified in their usual inane way. Protests would be mounted from abroad that his rights were violated and that he could not be assured of a fair trial in Panama.

Of course, they were right! So what! Had any of his victims been given a fair trial?

What a change in all of them over these past few years! Where Karena had a young daughter to contend with, she now had a young woman with all that involved. Oh boy! And the little guy, well, fortunately, he still wanted to be a kid! Whew! And she was back in her element. What a professor she would make one day, of that he had no doubt! As for him, well, he was pretty content. What a strange word to apply to him. It had been so very, very long ago when contentment was even in his vocabulary.

But things were different now. Justice, at least to a degree, would be served. His demons had been put to rest, he hoped. Maybe, just maybe, he could lead a normal life, whatever that meant.

It would take another 6 months, but then word came that Marcos was back in Panama, and in custody. And that his trial would begin in just a few months. Panamanians cheered and congratulated each other, and as if Panamanians needed any excuse for a party, they used this as an opportunity to add another holiday to their calendar, official or not!

49.

WELCOME TO CANADA!

Our man began to think of those back home in Canada. His kids, and other family, and friends he had left so long ago. For a guy notorious for keeping in touch, these past few years belied that fact. He wanted to go home. But not alone.

So he and Karena and the kids boarded that big bird and headed to the land of his birth. To say that she was afraid would be an under statement, yet she had no reason to be. After what they'd been through, this would be a walk in the park! Funny how family does that to you. They can build you up or tear you down with merely a few words being uttered!

This trip would tell the tale. There would either be many more trips to follow . . . or none. He suspected the former, and he would be right. They embraced them with open arms, as if they were long lost friends, and indeed they would become fast new friends.

The prodigal son had returned. His mother, ever feisty, would be first in line to greet them, and invite them into her home. So it would follow with his siblings. And his daughters, well, they couldn't wait! Where fear may have been, joy would soon replace it. Karena knew they were accepted and were now part of a much larger family.

And his friends, those who were real were still real, and they celebrated their homecoming, and the family became ever larger.

They would stay a month or more in this land of ice and snow and take back memories that would surely last a life time! But it was cold, oh my God, it was cold! But warm hearts can stand up to cold anytime, and cold held no power over them! Now it would be their turn to come down south. Plus 30 C every day, and feeling like 40, should be interesting. And in a few months, they would find out!

It seemed such a long time ago that he had grabbed that back pack and a one way ticket to anywhere. Anywhere but here! Many have asked him if he knew then what he knows now, would he have ever left?

And of course the answer is "YES!" Would he have made other choices, given the opportunity? Hell, ya! But yesterday is gone, and he, for one, was quite content to leave it there!

Advice for others? Do your homework. Figure out your comfort levels. Trust your gut. And get out of there if you don't feel comfortable. They are always watching you. Know that!

The one fear he had always had was this: what happens when everything is back to normal. I'm not used to normal. Very few of the people I know think I will survive "normal" and that bothers me. I don't want them to be right. She deserves more than that!

He had to admit that this life was different. Calm, peaceful. Just what everyone wants. Right?

So he tried to settle in. She's in University, the kids are in school, and he has all the time in the world to write and photograph to his heart's content. Financially, they were fine.

Yet as a trap yet unsprung waits for its prey, he also waited. For what, he knew not. But he would know when the time came. He sensed its approach.

He was right. When they knocked on his door, he knew his journey was far from over. He was being investigated along with others, as accomplices of Marcos. Now, they knew of his work and how he had been instrumental in bringing Marcos to justice, but they had to follow all the leads. You understand, amigo? Si, of course.

The days that followed would once again drive him to the depths of despair, and he would begin to doubt his own motives. The authorities had their doubts. She began to wonder how well she really knew this man.

On and on this would go. He certainly began to understand why people would confess to things they had not done just to get it over with! But he would not give them the satisfaction. Try as they might, they could not break this man. Besides, he had done nothing wrong! They knew it! But the pressure on them from above was relentless, and they needed bodies to parade through the streets. Well, his would not be one of them!

And it wasn't. Maybe he was just being paranoid, but Karena seemed to have her doubts, and that bothered him. After all they had been through, how could she still doubt him?

She didn't. Not one bit, but somehow he felt she did. A crack began to form where none had existed before. They began to pick at each other, that is, until her Mom read them the riot act! Funny, she used to be his biggest critic! With a few snaps of the whip, they were back on the same page! They both realized how fragile they still remained. They were healing but they weren't yet fully recovered. They were not the others' enemy! If there be a time to stand united it was now.

Soon the authorities grew tired of this man, and finally gave him his due. He was a patriot. "But we had to keep up appearances and scrutinize you the same as the others. You understand?" "Of course. You were only doing your job."

It is amazing that cynicism doesn't rule all our lives. It certainly could, and many would say, it certainly should.

50.

THE JOURNEY REMEMBERED

Our man had began his self-dubbed "journey of discovery" in Canada so very long ago. He had decided then that he would let his "gut" direct his path, wherever that may lead him. It took him to places he could not have envisioned, and to experiences that were unimaginable. In many ways it gave him life, and in other ways, it tried its best to snatch life itself from his hands.

He cared not what happened to him in the early days of this journey. He didn't purposely put himself in jeopardy, but he didn't avoid it either. He felt that he used common sense, at least as he defined it, in most of the situations he found himself in. Many would beg to differ, but that is their prerogative. The world came alive to him, and it mattered not where he went, and each and every experience would help to redefine this intrepid traveler.

When one travels alone, one's senses must become heightened because you are never really alone. There are watchers out there, and they are watching you. It's true.

One must never show fear, or be indecisive, for that would be folly. Many have become victims if they were not vigil. He should know, and his mistakes led him into a world unlike anything he had ever known. Even to be able to reminisce now about all the yesterdays seemed a miracle in and of itself. He should have been dead long ago.

But, he was very much alive and he would continue to reminisce, thank you very much. For he had done things, and met people from all over the world, and had experiences that a fiction novel could not match. And he had met her. For that to happen, a hundred other things had to happen first. And they did.

There was so much tragedy. He would be cast into hell, and yet pulled back from the brink before the fire could consume him. This would happen time and again. His faith would be tested over and over and where doubt may have existed, it existed no more. Despite the circumstances, he was able to find contentment in the darkest of the dark, and though uneasy, he knew he was not alone. Not alone! That would sustain him through the trials and tribulations that would befall him over the following years. Hard to believe how a few months odyssey had become a journey of a lifetime.

He had done a lot of crazy things way back then, and undoubtedly the worst decision was going to that "camp." That wasn't even him! What the hell was he thinking? Yet, if he hadn't, would he be here recounting this tale right now? Would his life have taken off in a whole new direction? Choices! Did he really have a choice? Supposedly, the thing that sets us apart was the right to choose. So God already knew the choice he would make and all that was to follow? Yes? Confusing, to say the least!

Yet he believed fervently that nothing happened by accident. Coincidences, please! Now, he would acknowledge that he had perhaps missed many opportunities that life had presented him along the way, or that supposedly things would be different if he would have zigged instead of zagged, and yet here he was. Here and now, and for whatever the reason, this is exactly the way his life was to have played out. Or was it?

And why her? It's not like he didn't get involved from time to time, but this was unusual, to say the least. To become involved in another countries politics? Please! To be a spy? He couldn't have made this stuff up if he tried! Yet, here he was. And all this thinking was giving him a headache!

He knew the months ahead would be difficult. Marcos' trial was set to begin and that would conjure up memories better left buried. For a nation, but also for him. Though he had moved on, he knew the fragility of the human mind. And he shivered.

51.

THE TRIAL BEGINS

The trial did begin. It would be long and arduous. The judicial system would live up to its reputation and more. Nothing, absolutely nothing could be taken for granted. Decisions taken bore no semblance to reality and in fact, one could not be certain that they were even at the right trial. Yes, welcome to a new Panama, the powers of the day would say. Yet nothing had changed and the people knew it.

Hope began to fade as quickly as their hopes had risen. It made no sense. This government had the support of the people and had been seen as harbingers of change. Why would they not grasp this opportunity?

Ricardo did try. He was a good man but he was in way over his head. His advisors, let alone Marcos, were more concerned about their own well being than the population at large.

This trial should have been the trial of the century down here. A watershed event that would put Panama on the map. A place to do business. Transparency would be a key ingredient of this government, yet, it appeared to all that absolutely nothing had changed. But it had, and slowly but surely Ricardo would wrestle power away from yesterday's men.

And though Ricardo may have been in danger of drowning, he had not. True believers began to make their voices known. And publicly back him up. The judiciary would be challenged as never before.

Even though they were part way into this trial, and some of the decisions were suspect at best, change was in the air, and decisions rendered today stood in stark contrast to decisions rendered yesterday. The population took notice and so did the world at large.

Could Panama really change? Beyond the promise stage? It appeared that a cautious "yes" may be the right answer after all.

Marcos had paid a lot of bucks to a lot of people to make this go away, but it became obvious that they may accept his money, and merely prove that they were as conniving as he. For a moment, just a moment, he thought that he may not get away with this. But that passed soon enough, and he reminded himself that he was superior to them in every way, and that soon victory would be his. Then watch out! Saddam thought likewise!

But there were scores to be settled that the "law" didn't know about. Well, actually they did, but that's another story. One by one the "contractors" would be hunted down and dispatched accordingly. There are no secrets once shared that remain secret. They may have just being doing "their job" but now others were doing theirs. And justice of sorts would be served.

No one would know, yet everyone knew. That's the way it works down here. Information would make its way back to Marcos, usually leaked by the government itself, to keep Marcos on edge, and it worked well. His necktie grew ever tighter, and he soon grew to distrust everyone around him. Paranoia became his friend, and comfort would befriend him no more.

But still, justice must not only be done, but "appear" to be done, for is not appearance more important than the actual? Sad but true.

Justice would be done. And as legions of his followers would soon know, crime and punishment can be two very different things. But remember, the appearance of justice is everything. The people rejoiced. With each and every conviction, confidence grew and Ricardo's popularity knew no bounds.

He had stayed the course and Panama was changing. Countries once scared, were approaching his government wanting to do business. He vowed to himself and God above that he would not weaken, that he would build on today and strive for excellence tomorrow.

He would gather strong and moral people around him. People with the same agenda as his, at least that was the plan. It would take every fibre in his being to pull this off for the pressure put on these people from the "outside" would challenge God himself.

Aaron would follow Marcos' trial religiously. At long last, it was his turn. He had sat through hundreds of hours of testimony, damning testimony that should unquestionably bury Marcos. But nothing down here could ever be taken for granted. As the trial drew closer to a conclusion, he found himself sleeping less and less.

As did she. He had come so far and yet she feared that the wrong outcome of this trial might just drive him over the edge. Again.

Would he ever forgive himself? He too was a victim yet he failed to see that. She grieved for her man. They had already gone through so much to be together and now they were in jeopardy again. She didn't know how much more of this she could take. How many times had they walked down this path? Far too many!

The jury had reached a verdict! Or did they? Would justice be done this day? There were many charges pending against Marcos, but this was the big one. Panama held its collective breath. And they together held theirs, and then it was announced.

"Ladies and gentlemen, we have a hung jury!" Silence. And then, it was if a bomb had went off, and there was wailing, and screaming, and chaos! Marcos smiled. Then he laughed! He laughed!

That would be his undoing. They could not hold the crowds back, and what was to follow would be spoken of in hushed tones for years to come. They attacked him as one, and at the end of the day this once powerful man was reduced to a shadow of his former self. A quivering mass of pulp and torn flesh was left as evidence; they would later say he had sustained multiple piercing injuries, 2 broken legs, crushed ribs, and in fact, they would say he died that day. And yet, he didn't. Once again he would survive. Thanks to a Doctor in the crowd that decided to uphold his Hippocratic oath!

So Marcos paid part of his debt that day. But it wasn't enough. As long as he lived, it would never be enough! Even though Aaron had dreamed of this day, he could not bear to watch the atrocities committed against Marcos in that courtroom. For evil itself rose up against evil that day, and there would be no winners. And the scars would remain forever.

This should have been the end of Marcos! But it wasn't! Ordinary men had risen that day and plunged themselves into hell! They had become Marcos!

Aaron and Karena made their way home that afternoon, nary a word spoken. What was there to say? Evil had won the day!

They were not hungry this night. They sat across from each other and each looked deeply into the eyes of the other. They knew not where to go with this. When they went to bed that night, they lay back to back, each wide awake. Each reliving the days' events.

52.

WE ALL LOSE

This was not a victory. In fact, it was a loss for everyone involved. The judiciary had exposed its open wounds for all the world to see. The trial was, at best, a sham. Jury rigging was merely business as usual. But what followed was unexpected, for the anger barely contained, was contained no longer.

Panama did not need this. And the world wasn't sure how much it needed Panama. Not that the "world" at large was any better, just that they hid it better.

So what now? A hung jury could have happened anywhere, could it not? Of course, but was that the problem? No doubt the system was still corrupt, but that did not explain the shocking display that followed the non-verdict. Ordinary people doing extraordinarily evil things, in front of the world, no less.

Ricardo would do the right thing again, if such even existed, and he addressed the nation, and the world. He would condemn the broken justice system and those who had taken the law into their own hands, and he would prosecute them to the full extent of the law. The law! What a joke! He knew it, but the appearance of justice was the thing. He asked his people and the world to not give up on Panama, but to join him in righting the wrongs of this nation. Again, the ordinary man on the street would come alongside him once more. This was a nation that wanted desperately to move forward, and they desperately wanted to believe that Ricardo was their man.

The nations of the world would stand as allies, for was it not in their best interest that Panama would rise from the ashes? This was a country rich in natural resources, and they were determined to be at the table.

Once again, Ricardo had proven that he was indeed the right person for the job. But now he would make changes. Big changes. The judiciary would be among his first victims.

What of Marcos? Swept away to a private hospital (which also contained a separate wing where they discreetly held political prisoners) at the governments expense no less, to heal. What the hell's wrong with this picture? They should have taken him to the gallows. Better yet, they should never have revived him! Maybe they should hang that Doctor instead!

Karena, too, was outraged and was quick to let it be known. She was certainly not alone. Panamanians en masse demonstrated in the streets but there was a sense that it was to no avail. The monster had not been killed. It began to look like he never would be.

The eyes of the world watched every move that Ricardo made, and it mattered not what he did or said. For he was Panama, and Panama had failed miserably. Yet he would not quit. That alone would set him apart from others that had gone before him. And though it would take time, the world would begin to appreciate this man, and begin to give him his due.

Panama began to slowly re-emerge yet again. Slow and steady it would be but ultimately it would become the place to invest in, a place known for its transparency. Soon, the money changers would return. Greed would find its way. It always does!

And Marcos? Had they just forgotten about him? Put him in file thirteen? Or what?

Aaron slowly slipped away from Karena. She had tried in vain to get him to open up, to talk to her. But it was if he had already left, and although he went through the motions of the day, she was afraid. Very afraid. They had walked this path so many times before, and they were so sure that it would be finally over, and yet, it wasn't. Again!

He tried to reassure her. He told her how much he loved her, and that he was fine. Just tired. Just didn't want to talk about it. But she didn't buy it for one second.

She tried to remember when they had ever been really happy. From the moment they had met, and throughout their entire history together, there had been turmoil. Rarely between them, but they were always operating in crisis mode. How they had ever made it this far was beyond the both of them. Actually they did know why. Crazy as it may sound, the simple truth was that they just really loved each other! And both felt that God himself had brought them together. Try telling that to most of the people they knew!

She knew him well. Very well. She knew he would not rest until Marcos lay in the cold, dark ground. And she knew he wasn't going to leave it up to the judiciary system.

Aaron knew what he had to do. He knew it might destroy Karena and him forever. But how could he let this monster go? He had had his chance! he had done the "right" thing! Right thing! And what had that accomplished?! But this time he would get it right!

He knew he couldn't talk to her about it. She would say she understood but she wouldn't really understand why he had to do this. "Why you?"

Why not him may be the better question? How could he have been so naive? Marcos was indeed the puppet master, and he had been the perfect puppet! Unforgivable! Unconscionable! He was supposed to just let it go? Impossible!

Karena's Mom had had it with these two! It sure was a lot easier in the early days when she was the one that wanted that gringo gone at any cost! She had to chuckle. He had come into their lives and she really liked him. What a nice guy! Karena had insisted that he was just a friend. He ate at their diner and they talked for hours. Then she found out how close they really were and banned him from her house. "Get out of our lives! You will only hurt her!"

Yet here she was. The peacemaker. Again. After what they had all been through these past years it was impossible not to believe that God had a plan for these two: together. These two loved each other passionately, but they were as stubborn as the day was long! So she would sit them down again, and remind them of a few things. Kids these days!

Of course, they knew she was right. As she delivered her sermon to them once again, Karena slipped her fingers through his and he pulled her close to him. They looked deeply into each other's eyes, and without a spoken word between them, they knew what they had to do. And they would. Together.

They both knew this would not be over until Marcos and his ilk had met their maker. And they were going to ensure that that was sooner rather than later!

He had never in his wildest dreams ever expected to be front and centre in another countries politics. He certainly didn't expect to be part of a covert operation that would take "down" anyone, let alone men like Marcos! Hell, he had never even expected to get "involved" with anyone seriously on this voyage of discovery!

For a brief moment it crossed his mind that he should write a book. But who would believe the stories he could tell? Hell, he lived them and they still didn't seem real!

How could he have known that all roads would lead to Karena? How could he know that God had a plan not just for his life, but for their lives? And how could he know that he would become so intimately involved in the life of a nation?

As strange as this seemed, he had never been more alive! And his purpose had never been more defined!

This tale was far from over. In fact, a new chapter was about to begin, but he and Karena would be as one. God willing, their love would sustain them when Satan himself came calling. And He was knocking on their door!

53.

MARCOS ARISES

Indeed he was! Marcos had many months to think. As he slowly regained use of his facilities, he could think of only one thing: he had let that son of a bitch live, and he had repaid him by turning him in! But he would pay! "Mark my words! I'm coming for you! I will destroy not only you but everyone close to you, starting with her! You're a dead man!"

Marcos was powerful even when contained, and they should have known that it was inevitable that he would one day walk among them again. He had powerful friends, and money would buy the rest. One day he would just disappear from that cell. They would try and hush it up, or say he had died, but it wouldn't be true. And though he may have failed in his task, revenge would be oh so sweet, and he knew exactly where to find them!

Sleep would not come to Aaron these days and he knew something was amiss. And though he confronted the authorities on every occasion that he could, their elusive answers gave him pause. This could not go on much longer. He and Karena had agreed that Marcos must be taken down once and for all. And yet she seemed reluctant. They had a good life now. Couldn't they just leave Marcos to the authorities? Maybe she could, but he couldn't.

Once again they would talk late into the night. Once again a decision would be made. He would go but he would stay in constant touch with her. No more secrets, no more disappearing acts! There was no other way! She loved him and was afraid for him but she understood what he had to do. So ironic, here he was, not even a Panamanian, yet more dedicated to their cause than most Panamanians! He loved her so. He wanted to stay so badly but he could not. Not until this was over!

Marcos had recovered rather well considering the extent of his injuries. But pain would be his constant companion from here on in. He relished it! It kept him focused on what he had to do! He was still locked up but that was just a technicality. He would soon take care of that little problem.

He had overthrown a nation. And this is how they had rewarded him. They would pay! Everyone would pay, but first, the gringo and his family! He would start with her and the kids, and he would make him watch! Then he would carve "his" gringo up until he begged him to die!

Aaron had bought his ticket to Canada a few days earlier, and had "arranged" for another to take his place. Not at all difficult if you know the right people. So now he had his "excuse" if he ever needed it. It couldn't be him; he wasn't even in the country! That's how it worked. They let it be known that he would be gone for a couple of months. Nothing unusual about that.

So he and his cohorts slipped away undetected and began the trek to, of all things, break Marcos out of prison. Crazy? Of course! But down here, graft is a huge weapon, and they had attained what they felt would do the job. There was much to be done, but they were more than up for the task. This had taken many months of planning, and unfortunately he was unable to include Karena in the initial stages, for she would have surely talked him out of it. In any case, this monster would soon be brought to justice. Just not in a courtroom!

Marcos knew it was time. He felt good. Good enough to get the hell out of here. Money can buy anything. And it did that night. So what if a couple of guards lost their lives. Big deal! Now I will have my revenge!

Their intelligence was confusing. Something was up at the prison but no one was talking. Try as they would, they could extract no information concerning Marcos. What the hell? Was he even there? Answers would not be forthcoming!

Karena called. She had been hearing rumours. Rumours concerning Marcos. Apparently he had escaped, yet the government was in denial. "No, he had not escaped. He was in a secure facility and being held away from prying eyes." That was the official version.and that's what they would stick with.

54.

I'M COMING FOR YOU

Marcos' friends urged him to get out of the country and regroup. Panama was too dangerous. Wasn't he proof positive of that? But he would have none of that! He had a little business he had to take care of first.

So despite their objections, under the cover of darkness, Marcos slipped into David. The gringo would soon be his, and if his info was solid, before this night was over, he would exact his revenge! He would make that son of a bitch watch as he carved up the kids, and especially her! And he would enjoy every moment of it!

When Karena contacted him, he knew that he was too late. He knew exactly what Marcos would do, and he gasped for air less he suffocate. "Oh my God!" He begged her to go! Now! Grab the kids and your Mom and get out of there now! Go to "our place." Wait for my call. And tell no one! She knew he was right and within minutes they were on the road.

"Please Lord, not my family! " Aaron was beside himself. Again and again and again! Marcos beat him every time! Now he was going after his family. To get him! And this little band of patriots would make their way to David this night as well. All he could do was "pray." Despite the circumstances, he chuckled to himself. "All I can do is pray!" For God's sake, what the hell had they relied on these past few years?

And so he would get back to business. They would head to their home and pray that Marcos had not gotten there first. He'd better call her one more time, just to be sure. And he did. But there was no answer. A chill ran through him. Maybe she hadn't got away on time. Maybe Marcos had her. If he did . . .

Marcos knew which neighbourhood Aaron lived in, and it wouldn't take long before someone would rat him out. Wave a few bucks in their face and they would sell their grandmother! And that's exactly what happened.

A neighbour down the street saw them coming and alerted Karena. That was all the time she needed. As soon as Aaron called she had grabbed what they needed, and she and the kids and her Mom were out of there. Immediately. And yet, almost too late! They had a long way to go. She could only pray that they had not seen her leave! She tried Aaron's cell again. Still no answer. "Where are you?"

Marcos and his men surrounded the house. It was unusually dark, but that would matter little. Marcos would own this night and the gringo would pay! Oh God, would he pay! He rubbed his hands together in anticipation. Even his own men would shudder at what was to come! Too late!!! Marcos was outraged! "If it's the last thing I do, I will get you and everyone close to you!" Their little home would light up the darkness that night. All that they had worked so hard for would be gone in an instant. As the flames did their work that night, Marcos' men could not help but notice the ominous shadows surrounding their leader. And they knew that evil was in their midst.

They could see the fire dancing above the tree tops, and Aaron felt sick to his stomach. Was that their house? In a few moments he would know!

It was. There were people milling about. They would tell Aaron of the strange men that had been there earlier and had torched the place. They would speak of the leader of this band, and how ungodly he appeared. And how he kept screaming Aaron's name! Then, they had just up and left.

Aaron was in a panic. She had made it out before Marcos got there but where the hell was she? Where was Marcos? And why wouldn't she answer the phone?

Why hadn't he listened to Karena and just stayed home? At least he would have been there to protect her and the kids. Now they were in mortal danger again because of him! How many times had he put them in harms way because of his bruised ego? What the hell was his problem? Why she stayed with him he did not know. That's not true. He did know. The same reason he stayed with her through everything. They believed in each other. Even her Mom was on board! And that was a miracle in and of itself! But, back to reality. Where the hell was she? Why didn't she answer her phone? "Please God, please . . . "

She was scared, and driving at night on these roads only made it worse. When the phone rang, she could only stare at it. Did she dare answer it? She didn't recognize the number. What if it wasn't Aaron?

"Hello." It was him! "Thank God. Where are you?" "At the house, at least what's left of it." "What do you mean?" So he told her, and he could hear her crying. That house had meant the world to her. What they had went through to get it, and then when he had disappeared for so long, it had served as a refuge for her and the children and now it was gone!

"Hon, we can build another house! We're alive! That's all that matters!" She knew that. Still . . .

There was no quit in Marcos, and he was fuelled by revenge. "I own you! You will be mine this night!" They had received word that a vehicle had been spotted just a few kilometres ahead driving erratically, with a woman at the wheel. Was it her? Soon enough they would know, and Marcos rubbed his hands together in anticipation. "The things I will do to you!"

Karena kept glancing back at the seemingly endless stream of headlights that were rushing up on her from the rear. She knew she had to do something drastic. Even if it wasn't Marcos, she couldn't take that chance. So she shut off all her lights, nearly giving her mom a cardiac, and slowed to a crawl making sure she didn't touch the brake pedal lest the brake lights came on, and made a slow turn down a country road. When she felt she was far enough away from the main road, she shut off the engine, and begged the kids to be silent. Then she prayed. And waited.

She watched them come, at least a half dozen vehicles, and then she watched them go. They were safe for now, if that was even Marcos, but now what? Then the phone rang again, and it was Aaron.

She let him know where she was, and her suspicions about the motorcade that had just passed by. He begged her to stay where she was and he made his way to them. Thank God they were safe! Well, not exactly safe, but at least Marcos didn't have them! They couldn't go home. Marcos had ensured that.

The government and the police force would spare nothing to find Marcos. Despite their best efforts, he was not to be found. Had he managed to get out of Panama yet again? The world watched. One man. Taunting a nation.

Aaron knew that Marcos would not leave Panama. Not this time. Even though the nation would search high and low for him, he would not be caught. Aaron grew afraid, very afraid. Marcos had nothing to lose and Aaron knew he was coming for him. It was inevitable that they would meet up, and probably very soon. Lord, please lead me to him before he can find us. Let's settle this once and for all!

It seemed that the only sensible thing was to get Karena and the kids and her Mom out of Panama until this was finally finished. He couldn't bear to think what would happen if Marcos got his hands on them. But she was having none of that! We are staying together and that's final! Boy oh boy, when she got mad! And he had to chuckle, and that always set her off!

The one thing they could agree on was that they couldn't just wait like sitting ducks for Marcos to make his move. They couldn't hide forever, and sooner or later, someone would turn them in. They had to leave the country until this was all over. If that ever happened. She had to agree with Aaron that they didn't want to spend the rest of their lives looking over their shoulders, or worrying every time the kids went to school or even out to play.

"Fine! Then let's go, but, all of us, including you!" She was adamant about that. She had lost him too many times before. Never again! Yet, she knew that he was right. And she was afraid. These last few years had taken their toll on this incredible woman, and even she felt, not defeated, but definitely weakened. After everything they had been through together to arrive at "nowhere" had sapped her strength completely. She had always had to be so strong throughout her life just to survive. Then he had come along, and for a brief time, she rested, at least a little, but that was so very long ago. But when he came home from Canada in such a fragile state, she knew she would have to dig even deeper, for he had breathed his very life into her, and she knew she would do the same for him. What a pair they were. Neither had given up on the other, despite all the crap thrown their way. She knew, as he did, that they had been brought into each others life for a reason, and that reason had manifested itself over and over these last few years. And here they were, and they were not done yet!

They weren't done. Not by a long shot! Instead of leaving Panama as they had intended, they decided to go to their "place." It had served them well in the past, and it was unlikely to be found. Besides, they could slip over to Costa Rica by water if it became necessary. So they settled in as best they could. They prayed that Marcos would be caught. Good God, how could he stay invisible forever? And yet, here they were, doing the exact same thing!

55.

GONE . . . REALLY?

Marcos had indeed left the country. He had sympathizers everywhere. Costa Rica would do nicely! At least for now. Until he had settled a couple of scores. Then he would get the hell out of here and regroup back in the good old USA. They thought they had him! Give me a break!

He had called on an old friend in Costa Rica whom he knew would provide for him. And he did. And once again, Marcos was living in style. Low key of course, but in luxury compared to the misfits he was planning on burying. Real soon.

He could slip in and out of Panama by boat any time, especially under the cover of darkness. He would bide his time, but the gringo would be his.

It was inevitable that they would meet. Ironically, they were but a few kilometres apart, Aaron and family on the Panamanian side; Marcos on the Costa Rican side.

Aaron did not handle boredom well, and this was boring! Yes, he was grateful to be with the people he loved but how anyone could just sit and watch the sun rise and fall everyday must be nuts! If this is what one is supposed to look forward to in retirement, then I never want to retire. And to think, this is what most of the world I come from wants. Unbelievable!

How much longer they could do this was anyone's guess, but as far as he was concerned, if they didn't hear something soon, they were going to get to Canada one way or the other. They could get used to the weather, after all, he had gotten used to theirs, now it would be their turn!

But today, fishing was on the agenda. Again. So they headed out to the open sea. They were usually alone out here but today was a little different. Lots of activity on the water. Maybe some researchers or something. Let's check it out.

Karena had waited for them to depart this day because she had something to do. And she knew Aaron would not approve. So she made the call. "Hola." "This is Karena." That's all it took. Yes, the Fighters had left her hanging. They had sided with Marcos. For a time. When they tried to get hold of her, she was not to be found. Yes, they would help her take down Marcos! She knew Aaron would be angry but they needed help, and help was now on its way. They would be there by morning and then they would, together with Aaron and Karena, put a plan together to dispose of that mad dog once and for all. The biggest job would be finding him, but they would, and then they would destroy him once and for all.

As the sun disappeared over the horizon, Karena wondered where Aaron and the others were. Unusual for them to be out this late. She had tried to reach him several times. Strange. He always had his phone with him. Always. She began to pace, and glance furtively towards the shore line. Now it was late and still nothing!

Her heart threatened to rip itself from her chest, but still she said nothing. Then the phone rang! Thank God! She hurriedly answered it "Aaron?" But it wasn't. Then she knew. And she collapsed, and her screams could be heard throughout the village.

"Aaron?" "Hello Karena." Then Marcos laughed uncontrollably. At last! They had surrounded those fishermen, just to check them out in case they were spies, and, lo and behold, it was his gringo! There was a God after all! He had delivered him straight into Marcos' waiting arms! He had almost given up finding him and had decided to head back to the U.S. But now it was Christmas time, and he was going to take his sweet time unwrapping the package! It was just a matter of time until he had his whole family! Oh happy days!

But what he had neglected to tell Karena was that the only part of Aaron that he actually had was his phone. They had taken them by force, and all three aboard the vessel had went overboard to avoid Marcos' men. It hadn't taken long to dispatch two of them, but Aaron was yet to be found. He was in the water, and his time was rapidly running out.

When he found the cellphone in their boat, he knew he would find the rest of them. Why not make the call? And he did, and soon they would all be his!

Perhaps! Perhaps not! Had he known Karena at all, he never would have made that call. If he thought she would wait around for him to appear, well, forget that! And within 30 minutes they were gone. She knew where to go. They had always had a plan "B" just in case. She cried uncontrollably as she drove; this nightmare was never ending it seemed. But she knew Aaron, and if there was a way for him to escape from Marcos, he would find it. But Marcos had his phone and was taunting her now, and she feared that her husband might well be dead. Please God! She knew that you don't bargain with God, but what could it hurt! Karena could take no more. Under protest she left her mom and the kids at the safe house. "Talk to no one! I'll be back soon." And she was gone. When she was safely out of their sight, she pulled the vehicle over, got out and retrieved the package she had hidden in the trunk. It felt strange in her hand. So long ago. But this was different. And she was ready. Well, Marcos might be looking for her, but what he didn't know, was that she was looking for him! She would find him and she wouldn't be coming alone.

56.

TOGETHER AT LAST

They had shot Manuel just as he went over the edge. He didn't stand a chance. Jose had taken a round to the leg but managed to get into the water. He was bleeding badly and he knew that the blood was bound to attract some company that he would have rather avoided. If he even lasted that long. Aaron had went overboard on the opposite side of the boat, and the boat took the bullets meant for him. So he was unhurt but in shark invested waters along with a buddy who was bleeding profusely. And men up above with guns.

Jose was in trouble, big trouble, and yet he waved Aaron away. God that was hard, yet there was nothing he could do. He watched Jose slowly break the surface, and he saw blood, lots of it, and he knew those bastards had shot him again. He knew what he had to do. So he filled his lungs as best he could, and he dove deep and headed straight for Marcos' boat. If he could make it to there, he might be able to hide in plain sight. And he did. Barely. He felt he could pass out but he hung on for dear life. Once again he was granted an extension. For how long? God only knows, and he wasn't telling Aaron!

They would search the rest of that day and into the night. He couldn't just disappear. He was here somewhere, and Marcos was determined to see his gringo in the flesh. But it didn't happen. And Marcos was angry. They all thought him dead. There's nowhere for him to go, and besides, there's sharks in these waters! But Marcos was unconvinced. "He has as many lives as I do. "He's alive! I know it!"

It had been over twelve hours since they had sent those men to a watery grave, and perhaps they were right, perhaps it was time to go home. Tomorrow they would find his family and finish the job. So Marcos reluctantly set sail for home, but he sensed that this was far from over.

At last they were moving. If he could just hang on a little longer. He couldn't believe that Marcos would under estimate him again! Hell, he would have checked under their boat immediately. Where else could he have gone?

When they had finally moored, Aaron was completely wasted. Any longer and he would have surely let go. He had been dragged through the water for over an hour and it was all he could do to just stay afloat.

They had posted a couple of guards at the yacht, but Marcos and gang had made their way up to the house. Marcos was furious and unconvinced that his "gringo" was really dead. And that bothered him.

It should have. Because Aaron was not about to let this opportunity pass. He had come too far, and was too close to back off now. It was a miracle he was even still alive. After tonight Marcos wouldn't be!

He was so tired, and so weak. And he was going to take down Marcos? He needed to rest; to think. If only he could contact Karena!

He had to get out of the water. Now. If they found him . . . he could only imagine. And he shivered.

He had noticed a small skiff just a few lengths over, and although risky, he needed to do something. So he ever so slowly swam so as not to attract any attention, and slipped over the side unseen. And he lay there. It seemed an eternity. He had surely drifted off and he awoke with a start. Dawn was threatening to expose him so he slipped ever so gently back into the water. He watched. And a plan began to take shape in his mind.

He knew Marcos would go after Karena, and if he took the yacht, then Aaron had full intention on being aboard. How? Then he knew what he must do. He had been watching the two "guards" and they obviously weren't happy with each other. They argued and pushed each other about and he knew that this was time to make it or break it. He slipped silently onto the deck and lowered himself into the life boat. He pulled the canvas tarp over him and prayed. If they ever checked that would be it!

He had been in many tight spots before but this was different. It was as if he were in a grave, above ground, and nowhere to go. So he waited, and he left the tarp slightly ajar so he could see, at least a little.

And finally, he saw him. Oh my God, if he were caught . . . But, he wasn't and the long wait would begin.

Off they set. Marcos and a half dozen men, all packing hardware. If I get out of this alive it will be a flipping miracle, he thought to himself.

They anchored several hundred meters from Aaron's home, and four of Marcos' men took the speed boat to the main land. Soon his family would be theirs. We need to get the hell out of here ! If they catch us in Panama we're screwed! Why couldn't Marcos just leave it alone! For God's sake, the gringo was dead. Leave his family alone! Yes, that's what they thought, but to cross Marcos? Forget it!

They would have been a lot better off if they had followed their own advice. And instead of them ambushing Karena and family, she and a few freedom fighters ambushed them instead and took their boat and headed for Marcos' yacht.

The life boat was well equipped and Aaron found a filleting knife. Looked brand new. Before this day was over, it would be well used if he had his way!

So he slipped from his grave and watched and waited. How long he had he did not know. Once they discovered that his family was long gone, they'd be back, and his cover would surely be blown.

Finally Marcos went below deck. Then there were two. On opposite ends of the yacht, AK 47's at the ready. Man, where was James Bond when you needed him? The absurdity of the situation made him laugh.

He flashed back to that camp of so very long ago. He remembered being horrified by what he saw. Those images still haunted him today and yet here he was, and about to . . . Could he even do it?

But he knew if he didn't, that they would never be safe as long as Marcos breathed. Nor would Panama.

He had watched their pattern for the last half hour and he knew that within moments they would be out of sight of the other for at least a couple of minutes. Not long, but long enough.

And then Aaron made his move. And when the blade sliced as through butter and not a sound was made, he knew he had entered another world. A world that he may never escape. With a gentle push, man and gun were sent to a watery grave.

Time was running out quickly and as he made his way port side, he could see the other goon hanging over the edge talking on his cell phone. That's all the time it would take. Soon he would join his buddy at the bottom of the sea. As he glanced towards shore, he saw a boat speeding towards the yacht! It was now or never!

Aaron was covered in blood, and he knew that even if he pulled this off, his hands would be forever stained. But now was not the time. He had come too far and only Marcos remained. And one of them would die this day!

And then he felt it. As he fell to his knees he knew that once again Marcos had the upper hand. As he pressed his hands to his side to stop the blood from spilling from his body, he thought of Karena and all they had been through.

He turned to face Marcos. And they studied each other. One, a Panamanian turned traitor; the other, a foreigner turned patriot for his adopted country.

Not a word was spoken as Marcos raised his weapon. Marcos had won and now he would finish the job! "Time to die, you son of a bitch!"

When the shot rang out he was surprised that he had even heard it. And his side hurt like hell. When he looked up, Marcos still had the gun pointed at him, but there was a strange expression on his face. And the blood flowed from his head and down his cheeks. What the hell?

Then Marcos fell to his knees and they starred at each other. Another shot rang out and Marcos fell over. And still he starred at him. Through lifeless eyes.

As Aaron slipped into unconsciousness he was sure that he saw her standing over Marcos, gun in hand. "Karena?"

EPILOGUE

Had there not been an infirmary on Marcos' yacht, Aaron would have surely died. Ironically, Marcos had saved him. Poetic justice or God's sense of humour? Take your pick.

The government would turn on its' heroes and brand them fugitives. They would be forced even further underground. The freedom fighters would begin to actively recruit, and there would be no shortage of takers. The Indigenous would come along side. Ill winds would blow across this land, and there would be no peace.

And then President Ricardo summoned Aaron.

THE END

DD ANDER BIO

DD ANDER never did fit in very well in the prairie town he grew up in. While his classmates were settling down to careers and raising families, he was dreaming of mountain peaks and tall ships. And though he would attempt to follow those dreams, he always ended up back home on the prairies.

For a good part of his life he stayed the course, but eventually, he took his leave. He travelled extensively, and his experiences would soon catch up with his passion for a different life.

It would take him into places he should not have trod, and into experiences he should not have had. Stories would be told, by him, that he would deem fiction, but those who knew him, knew not where the fiction ended and the truth began. And they dared not ask.

He began to blog regularly during this time. Hundreds of blogs would follow, and to those who knew him well, it became obvious that the greater story lie between the lines. The public story was there for all the world to see, the other, for certain eyes only.

Although he lives in another part of the world today, he is always close by in one form or another. Whether through his blogs, his photos, his novels, both fiction and non-fiction, or his one on one conversations, he is never very far away.

www.ingramcontent.com/pod-product-compliance
Lightning Source LLC
Chambersburg PA
CBHW070007260626
47159CB00005B/1709